# Dauntless Spirit

# Dauntless Spirit
## The Journeys of Elizabeth Kellogg, a Forgotten Indian Captive

The Republic of Texas

Indian Territory

Red River

Arkansas Territory

Louisiana

Comancheria

Trinity R.

Nacogdoches

Natchitoches

Parker Fortress

Brazos R.

Navasota R.

Neches R.

Washington

Montgomery

Sabine R.

Colorado R.

Harrisburg

Guadalupe R.

Gonzales

San Felipe

San Antonio

Victoria

Galveston Island

Velasco

Mexico

Rio Bravo

Gulf of Mexico

## Story and Illustrations
### by Betsy Wagner

*Families are mysteriously ubiquitous. Families have members that span the full range of possibilities. That is true in the case of the humans in this story — the humans in my family, the humans in the Parker family and the humans in the Indian families. In the process of making this book, I was blessed to have collaboration with my cousin, Tricia Duyfhuizen, the best partner, editor, publisher and advisor a writer could have.*

Betsy Wagner
P.O. Box 974
Columbus, Texas 78934

spiritofgonzales@att.net

ISBN 978-0-578-80551-1

Cover map, published 1838 by H.S. Tanner
Courtesy of the Dave Rumsey Map Collection

# Timeline for the Journeys of Elizabeth Kellogg

# Introduction

In the fall of 2019 a teacher used my first book, *Spirit of Gonzales*, as part of her curriculum in a Texas history class. I met with the students, and they asked me, "What happened next?" It was their innocent and sincere curiosity that led to the research and writing of this book.

I investigated the names of the family members who survived the Texas Revolution and the Runaway Scrape. The name of Clara Elizabeth Duty Kellogg surfaced only in connection with the Comanche raid on Fort Parker in May of 1836, the same raid in which the now famous Cynthia Ann Parker (mother of Quanah Parker, the last great Comanche war chief) was abducted. One of the five members of the Parker family who were taken in the raid was named Elizabeth Kellogg. Was this captive really the same Elizabeth Kellogg who lived in Gonzales and lost her son at the Alamo? In my research I found statements from other researchers who believe she was.

The following story is a fictional suggestion using facts pieced together to give the best answer I could find about "what happened next?"

# Part One:
# Planning a Journey

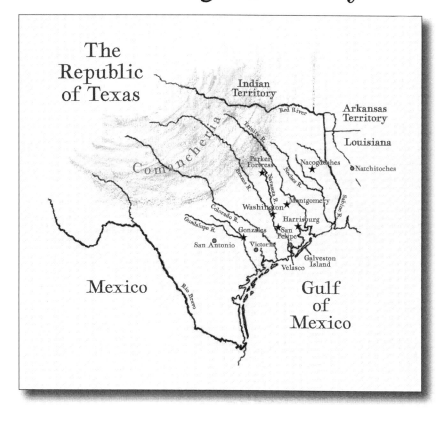

## Harrisburg, Texas—May 3, 1836

The dirt trickled into her hair and slowly filled the crevices of her face. Shovel after shovel, Benjamin let the soil slowly flow from the blade of his shovel as tears washed over his cheeks. He clinched his jaw and kept shoveling until there was a mound of dirt and nothing of her body was evident anymore. It was hard duty. This young woman loved his son, and she was the mother of Benjamin's only grandchild. It fell to him to set her into the earth.

"Rest in peace," a man said as he handed Benjamin Kellogg a small cross made of slender sticks of oak. The trees were burned, and small bits of wood had been salvaged by this pastor for the crosses he knew folks would be wanting now. So many graves needed them. The Methodist circuit preacher came to Harrisburg to offer any help he could, and this cross was a token of his condolences.

Without any words, Benjamin took the cross. Tired from the digging and the filling, he squatted at his knees, resting on his boots. He drew in a deep breath and blew it out his mouth.

Benjamin epitomized the typical Texas settler. His big hands were rough as pine bark and strong as Mexican huisache. Considered a "big" man because of his heavy bones, he carried very little extra flesh. Muscle, that's what he carried on his fifty-year-old frame. Benjamin stood short of six feet. Maybe his impact was more because of his demeanor. Quiet but unintimidated. And smart. He could fix anything. What was too broke to fix he would remake. The man was amazing that way. For whatever the reason, he left a big impression.

And he didn't abide waste. He considered hair a waste because it got in his way and cost him time if it got too long. He chopped his off with his razor about once a month when he was scratching back his beard. His tight curls helped delay the necessity for the haircut, but the facial hair was straight as pine needles. Those had to go pretty regularly, and if they didn't it annoyed him.

He'd kept himself trimmed up the last few weeks. Every day began with sharpening his razor on the strap as soon as he could see it. Any work he could do took his mind off his problems. Burying family was an emotional task, and he was trying to approach it administratively. It wasn't what he wanted, but at least it was work.

This morning as he sat at the side of her grave, Benjamin's long shovel rested in the crook of his elbow, and his hands came together in front of him, holding the little cross. He rubbed the leather strap that held the crossed pieces together. The pastor squatted next to him. "Who was it?" he asked.

"My daughter-in-law," Benjamin said as he twisted the vertical base of the cross into the loose dirt. "She tried so hard. She just couldn't make it any further."

The pastor sighed deeply. There was nothing he could say that would help, and he knew it.

As Benjamin squatted again for one last reflection, a bird lighted on the cross. It was a male cardinal, red as an apple and sociable as a best friend. But even he had an affliction. One of his eyes was injured. Ruined, maybe. He tilted his head and looked squarely at Ben with his one good eye.

Ben nodded toward the bird. "Everything's been wounded by the war," he said.

The friendly little bird jumped down onto the mound of dirt. He looked up, sang out a few chirps, picked up a straggling bit of straw and flitted away.

General Houston sent some of his men here from San Jacinto, sent them back here to Harrisburg expecting to find the town where the army supplies were stored. They came, not knowing Harrisburg was burned and the supplies were wasted. But as good soldiers do, they had already begun their work. With hammers and saws and the chorus of men's voices, they rectified the destruction Santa Anna left behind. Theirs were the first notes of recovery that would crescendo into the full harmony of reconstruction. But on this day the soldiers could only organize the destruction and account for the dead patriots who held Harrisburg for as long as they could before Santa Anna's raid.

The soldiers would have helped, but Benjamin didn't want help. He knew they had other work, and his duty was private. He and his wife valued privacy. In fact, he had come here for this task before most of the others were awake. He believed in getting his work done as soon as possible, and certainly burying Sydnie was something he wanted to be done and over.

It was an orderly procedure, this clean up by the soldiers. They made a roster and wrote as much identification as they could find for the dead. Some had papers to identify them. A letter in a man's pocket read, "We love you dearly, Adam," signed by someone named Amy. Another had a voucher for money he was owed. "James Erwin is owed seven dollars for the loan of a saddle to the Army of the People of Texas." Some were known by their friends who survived and came back to take up the work. If information was known, it was written on the roster. Unfortunately, many were just a number with some description. "Number thirty-four, thumb missing on the right hand." Or "Number twenty-eight, jagged scar over his left eye."

A large community of dead bodies was awkward. They would be a distraction, so they took the first order of business. The unclaimed and unknown were dragged away from the main camp, their souls lifted to heaven in purifying flames. In that early season of grief, John Benjamin and Elizabeth Kellogg would see that Sydnie was laid in the grave she deserved. Hard duty as it was, Benjamin would do right by her.

Her grave was down by the bayou. Others were there, so she wouldn't be alone. They were strangers, yes. But mingling with strangers in Texas was commonplace. Even in the afterlife, surely it would be a comfort to have a community—even if strangers—lying together in peace. There had been enough violent disagreements.

For at least two years the people of Tejas had struggled with the animosity, the misrepresentations and Mexican aggression. The contest out on the San Jacinto River declared the Texians "champions"—at least for a while. Many wondered if it was really settled or if this was just another of so many on-going battles.

These in the ground had found something in common. Death was what they shared. There would be no more arguments among them.

The pastor quietly got up, put his hand on Benjamin's shoulder and then walked away, leaving Benjamin with his thoughts.

Benjamin's wife Elizabeth couldn't go to the burial. She told Sydnie goodbye yesterday when they wrapped her in the blankets there on the ground. She couldn't watch as he dragged the bundle away, bewildered by her doubts and confusion. How had life gone so wrong?

So while Benjamin did this final act, Elizabeth stayed in the main camp, clinging to the memory of better times.

Elizabeth Kellogg appreciated solitude. Not that she didn't enjoy talking with people, because she certainly did. But she was most comfortable as an observer of life. She preferred her people one at a time.

Benjamin left her sitting alone on a broken buggy bench, one of the few useful remnants that survived Santa Anna's destruction. The buggy bench was secured to the boardwalk in front of the temporary storehouse the army had built. The storehouse faced the north and had a wide roof to cover the front porch. She felt comfortably invisible, tucked into the discreet little bench, waiting for Ben to return from the cemetery.

Discounting her own tatters, she took notice of the women gathering there. Torn, staggering, famished. With shredded dresses and dirty faces, they passed by. Some held the hands of children. Others were only able to walk with the support of their children. A woman passed by hobbling with a cane, her little son clinging to her skirt. They were both barefoot. *A widow?* Elizabeth wondered as she tucked her booted feet under her skirt.

Elizabeth had shoes. Good shoes. Leather boots that laced just above her ankles. They had belonged to her daughter-in-law, Sydnie. But a girl who is too sick to walk doesn't wear out her shoes. So Benjamin — refusing to waste them — had removed Sydnie's shoes, and Elizabeth inherited them. The shame she felt for wearing a dead girl's shoes was only part of her bewilderment.

Elizabeth searched the faces of the women who passed. Surely some-one she knew from Gonzales was there, but no one looked familiar.

*Where is Mary Millsaps?* she wondered. Mary was a blind woman with seven children. Her husband never came back from the Alamo. *Who is helping her now? Probably those seven children,* she thought. Eliz-abeth reminded herself how important it was to have children.

Elizabeth seldom missed the details around her. Most of those details were humans and the work of humans. But as she watched the people, a brave little bird landed on the crossbeams of the wide roofing over her head. The little feathered creature was building his own home, tucking some straw into the joint where the wood came together. She recalled an omen her mother had told her. The legend claims if a red bird comes to visit it means a loved one is watching from heaven. This bird was red. And Elizabeth noticed the poor thing had only one good eye.

## Meeting Charlotte Mexia—Morning May 3rd

"Pardon me, ma'am. Could I sit here with you a while?" A woman's voice drew Elizabeth out of her thoughts.

The small woman was strikingly beautiful. Her pale skin was a stark contrast with a thick crop of coal black hair twisted up on the back of the woman's head. Her clothes were from somewhere Elizabeth had never been. They were not from the wardrobe of a desperate pioneer,

and they didn't look like anything Elizabeth had seen in the United States. Her skirt was leather, falling mid-calf. Peeking out from under the skirt was a pair of fine boots. Those boots had the look of a recently plowed field. Deep scratches pushed over tiny rows of leather grain where they had been tested by hard wear. But the leather was still thick, evidence of its quality.

The woman's style was finished off with what was once a white blouse. What Elizabeth saw was a grubby garment, smudged with mud, grass stained and lined in crevices with grit. The crisis of the times in Texas had neutralized the population. This was a woman of means, but her social status had not protected her from suffering.

"Yes, please join me here, ma'am." Elizabeth said, tucking in her calico skirt.

She left as much room as she could and patted the space next to her on the bench. The two women together didn't take the space of a single parlor chair, slim as they were. They took their comforts and settled in.

As the dark-haired woman sat down, Elizabeth noticed a man standing just off the way, watching them. He was a bronze, swarthy man wearing a broad-brimmed straw hat the Mexicans called a sombrero. The man's clothes seemed a size too small. Elizabeth imagined the clothes having been damp and shrinking on to him, hugging his lean form as they dried. When he turned sideways, affected by a halo from the morning sun, he looked like a parenthesis, just a thin, slender line from his head to his toes.

As the woman settled herself on the bench, the man in the sombrero turned and walked across the road. Elizabeth detected a metallic jingle as he stepped away. He squatted on one foot under the singed skeleton of a tree that had escaped complete incineration. He positioned himself so that he continued to watch the ladies.

"My name is Charlotte Mexia." The woman took off a fine leather riding glove and offered her hand to Elizabeth.

Elizabeth took the outstretched hand and embraced it warmly with both of hers. "I'm Elizabeth, ma'am. Elizabeth Kellogg."

"I thank you," Charlotte said gesturing to their sitting space. She looked around at the mud and piles of debris that surrounded them. Then she looked back at Elizabeth. Charlotte put her hand to her chin. "What a disaster," she said.

Elizabeth nodded her agreement and tucked her skirt under her knees. She looked away at the rubble and checked the tightness of her hair bun. The sun was rising in the eastern sky, and Elizabeth squinted against it.

"Are you okay?" Charlotte asked. "Are you on your way back home somewhere?"

Elizabeth looked down the road at the camp sights and piles of debris. "I'm okay," she said. "I'm alive." She looked back at Mrs. Mexia. "That's a might more than some." Elizabeth felt herself wanting to remember Sydnie's smile and the sweet smell of her new grandson. She hoped to deflect the pain of that wanting, so she concentrated on Charlotte's chocolate eyes and asked her, "Do you have family around here?"

"Yes, I have family, but not here. They are far from here just now." The women were both quiet.

Elizabeth was thinking what a good thing to be far from here. She wondered how far a person would need to be not to be hurt by what just happened in Texas. She wanted to share her own family story, but it was too hard to tell; it was too complicated.

Charlotte continued, "Seems like everything is out of order now. But surely, with the new Republic, surely things will come back together for us all soon. Don't you feel that way?"

Before Elizabeth could reply a robust man approached the ladies on the bench. "Mrs. Mexia, it'll be a while. The axel broke. They'll fix it, but it'll take a while. I'm afraid we'll be here over night, ma'am." The man removed his hat with one hand. The other hand was wrapped in a cloth stained with blood. He held it down and tried to conceal it, but the bandages were too obvious.

"You've injured yourself, Tom!" Charlotte said.

"It's nothing, ma'am."

"Tom, that looks bad. Please take care of it." She stood up, reached out toward him and looked around for where he might go for help. "Tom, we can't have you getting a crippled hand. Does it pain you?"

"No, ma'am. It don't hurt none. Don't you worry, it's really nothing. There'll be something for it back at the wagon. I'll pour some whisky on it. Don't you worry none. We'll have you out of here tomorrow."

"Thank you, Tom. I know you'll do the best you can. You take care of your hand."

Tom replaced his hat and backed away a few steps. Tom looked like a man who knew a barber. He was slick-shaven, and his hair had style. In fact, there was style all over Tom. His shirt of beige linen had a bib held on with a double row of bone buttons. That shirt was tucked into dark canvas breeches. The legs of those breeches dipped into a pair of black boots that came to his knees. "I'll find you a place to spend the night," he said as he walked away.

Charlotte put her hand to her throat and breathed in so deeply the tattered blouse strained at the buttons. She watched Tom as he crossed the road.

Elizabeth watched Tom too. Much to her curiosity, she saw that he went directly to the wiry bronze man squatting by the tree. They exchanged a few words, a few gestures, and the man called Tom walked away.

Harrisburg was the town first designated "capital" of the Republic of Texas. That was the decision of the men at the convention held just eight weeks ago in Washington, Texas out on the Brazos River. The soldiers had already made rows of the waste that used to be a good-sized town before Santa Anna burned it down.

Today the capital was in Velasco, down on the Gulf Coast. The designation of "Capital of the Republic" would follow Interim President Burnet until things settled down—if they ever would. Harrisburg was just a reminder of "El Degüello," the music Santa Anna played to his enemy just before he murdered them, his anthem of no quarter, no compassion.

He came here to capture the leaders of the rebellion—Sam Houston, President Burnet, Stephen Austin, or whomever he might take. In his pursuit he had literally blazed his trail with fire from San Antonio to San Jacinto. Harrisburg was only one stop along the way.

Back in March, after the Alamo and before the final battle on the San Jacinto River, the Texians had stored precious supplies in Harrisburg, and Sam Houston left some of his men there for guards. Mr. Gail Borden was printing news tabloids to announce the declaration of independence signed in that meeting out in the Texas village called Washington. The first, fresh copies were right there on the printing machine when Santa Anna's men came into the newspaper office. Those freshly printed papers told him the truth, and it infuriated him.

The truth was that Burnet and his emergency cabinet of advisors had only hours before left for Galveston. Their departure was so recent the ink was barely dry on the papers. Santa Anna might have even seen the tail hairs of President Burnet's horse, snagged on a branch still waving in the wind. In realizing it, the general lost all reason.

Santa Anna might have benefitted his troops with a night of rest in the supply houses. He might have used the supplies and turned it all to his advantage, but no. He was a man who lived by rage and revenge, a narcissist who needed to show off, even if at his own expense. Showing his force was more important than the welfare of his troops. And so they dumped the presses in the bayou, torched the town and went on after the Army of the People.

But today as Elizabeth sat talking to Charlotte Mexia, the tables were turned. Santa Anna was held captive. About three hundred surviving members of his defeated troops were somewhere near Victoria, headed back to Mexico. Over six hundred Mexican bodies were left to rot unattended out on Peggy McCormick's farm field, while the victorious Texians were cleaning up the burned remains of Harrisburg.

"Mrs. Kellogg, do you have family here with you?" Charlotte focused her attention on Elizabeth.

In her usual way, Elizabeth wanted to be clear yet concise. She didn't waste her words any more than she would waste a ham hock. She looked at Charlotte and put a finger up to indicate that she was about to reply. She bought herself some thinking time by adjusting her skirt again.

"Well," she started, "yes . . . it's like this . . ." Elizabeth looked past her companion, into the space beyond them, out toward the bayou. She wanted to choose her words exactly right. "My husband, Benjamin . . ." The reality of what she needed to say lodged in her throat, and for the moment she felt she couldn't speak. She looked at Charlotte, and the two women locked eyes. They both knew this was a serious time, even if one didn't yet know the details of the other's story. Charlotte sensed Elizabeth's pain.

"Tell me, dear. Where is your husband?"

Slowly and quietly, Elizabeth formed the words she had not yet allowed herself to say. "He's burying our daughter." She nodded in the direction of the bayou.

There. It was said. She might be able to explain better at some other time, but for now, that was all she could say. If she had misrepresented the relationship by calling Sydnie her "daughter" so be it. That was more comfortable than trying to explain it. After all, Sydnie was the only "daughter" Elizabeth ever had. She reasoned that claiming her that way would have to do for now.

Charlotte's shoulders crumpled a bit, and she let a lot of air out of her lungs. "Oh," she said in a whisper. "I'm so sorry."

Elizabeth looked down and let unexpected tears flow. She didn't like being weak, but Sydnie had been her strength, and now even that was gone. Charlotte slipped an embroidered handkerchief out of her waist band. "I'm sorry to upset you." She put the fine linen cloth in Elizabeth's hand and curled their fingers together to indicate the gift.

Elizabeth accepted it and wiped her face. As she looked up, she saw Benjamin stepping toward them. He looked haggard but determined as always. He rolled a section of tree trunk to use as a stool, propped himself on it near the place where the ladies sat, pulled out his own handkerchief and wiped his face and neck.

"That's done, 'Lizabeth." He leaned back and took a deep breath. He looked at Charlotte. Elizabeth thought he wanted to say more, but he didn't.

"Benjamin, this is Charlotte Mexia," she said, nodding in the direction of her bench mate.

Benjamin stood and tipped his hat. "Ma'am . . ."

Charlotte nodded in his direction. "I'm so sorry for your difficulties, Mr. Kellogg." She looked down the row of rubble. "Trouble is all folks know these days."

Just as Elizabeth was thinking over their personal degree of trouble, the man named Tom reappeared. "We'll make a camp, Mrs. Mexia. There's plenty room for our wagon, and we'll unpack all the supplies while they see what needs doin' with that broken axle. The sergeant says a grub line will be formin' up in about an hour. I'll come get you later."

"Thank you, Tom. That's just fine, I'll be right here."

"Axel? You got axel trouble?" Benjamin asked.

"Yes-sir, she's just plumb broke. The Army has parts, but they too busy just now. We'll get it, jus' have to wait a spell."

"Let me take a look. Can you show me?" The two men struck up a conversation as they walked away.

"Your husband is very kind to offer help."

"He's not one to sit for long. He'll sleep better tonight if he fixes something today." Elizabeth explained.

"My husband will appreciate that. My Anthony is sailing. He can keep a boat afloat, and he makes business deals. He's away from me so much of the time, he hired Tom to drive my wagon."

"Away?" Elizabeth tried to imagine how it would be to have a driver and not have Benjamin with her at such a difficult time. She began to think about the exceptional boots, the leather skirt, the gift of a fine linen handkerchief and a private driver.

As Charlotte told about her sailor-husband, Elizabeth was distracted. She took notice again that the man in the sombrero was still watching them. Her curiosity grew with the image of Charlotte's driver talking to him earlier.

"Excuse me, Mrs. Mexia. That man over there keeps watching us." She pointed across the road to where the man in the sombrero leaned against the charred tree. "With all the work around, I wonder why he isn't working. Why would he just stand there and watch us?"

"Oh, that's my Chico! Anthony hired him to be on guard. Watching is what he does. Here, let me call him over and I'll introduce you."

Charlotte Mexia waved her hand toward the little man she called Chico, and immediately he crossed the street and came to her. She introduced them. Chico gave a salute of sorts, linked his hands respectfully behind his back, bowed a bit, and returned to his station across the street. Elizabeth tried to sort it all out. This new friend was not the typical farm wife Elizabeth had known in Gonzales or one of the desperate women on the 'scrape. After some thought Elizabeth decided Charlotte's differences were refreshing. "So many things happening, having someone watching out for protection must be a real comfort!" she said.

They smiled and almost laughed, though laughter was rare that day. And with that reassurance Elizabeth and Charlotte settled into their seats on the bench and watched the men working to clean up Harrisburg.

## Chico Leads the Way—Noon May 3rd

"Come now, señora, the food, it is ready." Chico came from across the road, carrying his sombrero in a roll, waving it excitedly. His black hair was thin across the top of his head. It was parted in the middle of his scalp and braided down the back of his neck. Something musical clanged as he walked. "The soldiers, they make a mess. The food is ready." He ran excitedly up to the bench.

"Gracias, Chico," Charlotte said, turning to Elizabeth. "Shall we go?"

"Oh, I don't know. I need to wait for Benjamin."

"Chico, Mr. Kellogg is with Tom back at the wagon. Would you go find them and tell them we're going to the mess camp?" Charlotte asked her guard.

Chico pulled himself together and stood with his hands in front of him, holding the sombrero at his chest. He looked at Elizabeth. "That what you want, Lady?"

"Yes, thank you, Chico." Elizabeth said as she stood up and stepped away from the bench. "I just want to be sure he can find me."

"Sí, señora. I bring Mr. Tom and Mr. K-logg to the mess camp. You just walk there . . . ." He pointed to the path the soldiers made alongside the piles of rubble. "Jus' follow the ruins, jus' follow the wasted houses." He gestured and jutted his hands out and danced a bit, trying to lead them in the right direction.

As Chico walked ahead of the ladies, Elizabeth realized the jangle of his gait came from a large, ornate silver spur — only one — worn on the man's left boot.

"Gracias, Chico. We'll find it." Charlotte waved her glove to her keeper. "You've done a good job. We'll meet you and the men somewhere near the mess camp. We'll all have a good dinner today, and you don't have to cook."

The wiry man grinned.

Leading the women along the pathway, Chico walked backwards and sidewards, turning and skipping as he went along. Finally, the sombrero was unrolled, and he pulled it down on his head again. "I go now. I come with Mr. Tom and Mr. K-logg," And he was off.

"He's quite a character, isn't he?" Elizabeth remarked.

"Oh yes, he's a rare gem." Charlotte stood watching as Chico left them. "He's been such a blessing," Charlotte said with a smile.

The path to the mess camp was edged with the waste of Harrisburg. The men and mules had pushed and pulled the burned wooden buildings into hills of charred lumber. It was all there on the side of the road, mixed with the remains of furniture and housewares. Stumps of chair legs jutted out. There was a broken pushcart, the partial frame of a window with a tattered curtain flapping in the early spring breeze.

During the past few days as they looked around Harrisburg, the Kelloggs wondered aloud what Gonzales might look like now. They knew they would return, eventually. Their little grandson was waiting there. They delayed their return hoping the baby's mother, Sydnie, would recover here in Harrisburg. But she couldn't recover, and now their choices were ambiguous.

Benjamin knew there is something soothing about spending time with the people who have known you forever. Hearing the same voices that were the first voices you ever heard, that is a comfort. He had suggested that Elizabeth would benefit from a visit to her family.

Elizabeth's family had a fortification deep in wild territory, on the prairie off the Navasota River. She spent time there a few years back while Benjamin worked out their homestead in Gonzales. That fortress had been standing strong and had proven to be steadfast for several years now.

Elizabeth always wondered why her family chose such a remote site, so wild and so far removed from other villages. The Duty-Parker family fortress was very near the terrible Comancheria. With the Indian troubles of the day, it was a very curious choice for a white settlement. But somehow the family had gotten along with the Indians, and it had worked out well . . . so far.

## Everybody Needs Help — Noon May 3rd

The clan out in the Parker family compound put their first Texas roots deep into the soil. Like a pine grove in the eastern regions of Texas, this family sowed a wide patch. They brought more than twenty wagons from Illinois, all in one swoop, people of faith, a whole church full. Elizabeth knew if she could find them again she could rest in the safety of that fortress. She agreed with her husband that spending time with her mother and sisters would be a sweet holiday. But should she go there or go back to Gonzales to be with the baby? The Parker place was one hundred fifty miles north of Harrisburg. Gonzales was one hundred forty miles west.

The two women walked on through Harrisburg. Working camps were to their left, hills of rubble on their right. People in desperate conditions walked along and passed them going in every direction. Men along the way gave serious attention to their duties, nodding at the ladies when appropriate.

"Oh, look at that," Elizabeth gasped as they passed a crowd of people lying on the ground. It was the sick bay, the clinic, the hospital. It was the gathering place for the diseased and injured. Men leaned on crude crutches, and their bandages sagged away from their limbs. She put her hand with the handkerchief over her mouth and nose to stave off the stench of gangrene and death.

Elizabeth remembered the army camp in Louisiana where they finally stopped running from Santa Anna. She remembered the desperate orphans she witnessed in that refugee camp just across the Sabine River where they waited to hear the news from the Texian troops. She felt even more determined to get away from this place and go to her family, if only she could. Fighting off a sense of guilt she turned her eyes away and thought, *Keep walking, Elizabeth. You've done all you can. You couldn't save Sydnie, and you can't save them. If you can save yourself, let that be enough. Just keep walking.*

"Oh, pardon, ma'am…" Elizabeth realized she had collided with another woman who was looking the opposite direction. The big blue eyes of a golden-haired child looked up at Elizabeth. Those eyes were full of tears, and the little nose was red and runny.

"Oh, Mommy, it hurts," the little girl whimpered. She pulled her arm down and held it in the skirt she had tucked between her little legs.

"Ma'am, what happened to her arm?" Charlotte reached out to the child as she spoke to her mother.

"We fell into some nettle," she said. The tearful little girl lifted her own arm to show Charlotte a rash. She had scratched it raw.

"It was dark, and we couldn't see our way," the mother explained.

Charlotte and Elizabeth realized the mother's neck was covered in angry little blisters.

"Come with me," Charlotte said. "I can get you something that will help."

The child looked up at her mother with pleading eyes. "Oh, thank you, ma'am," the mother said, looking back at the sick bay, as if she was glad to avoid the place.

"Come get some food, and I'll get a salve for your skin," Charlotte told her. The rash-covered woman nudged the little girl toward the food line, and the child sniffled. Together the four of them walked on toward the smell of beef.

"That food smells really good, doesn't it, Elizabeth?" Charlotte pointed in the air and forced a smile. She winked at the little girl.

They passed a few more camps and followed the aroma of food. A line was forming, and they fell into place at the end.

While they waited Elizabeth took notice of the people around them. There were more women with their children, barefoot and wearing ragged clothing, some with bandages, all with desperate faces. There were men, some in the uniforms of militia from the United States, but mostly just men wearing the tattered clothes of a pioneer farmer-turned-soldier-turned-survivor. She thought some of them must have been in Gonzales, with that mob waiting for Sam Houston just a few weeks ago.

"Beef stick, ma'am?" A man with rope suspenders over a bare chest interrupted Elizabeth's thoughts, as he presented a chunk of beef. It was pierced through with a stick, and the juice ran down the man's hand.

"Oh, yes. Thank you," she said. She took the stick in both hands and handed it to the rash-covered mother.

"Thank you, ma'am," the woman said as she bent over to give her daughter the first bite.

"Corn mash in the pots. Just not 'nuf dishes yet, ma'am. They'll be comin' on later."

Elizabeth remembered the plates, the cups, and the platters hastily thrown into the pits they dug in Gonzales. She had just seen broken bits of pottery on the path alongside the chars of wood on her way to the mess camp. Santa Anna had made life more difficult but not impossible. "Thank you, sir," she said as she squared her shoulders and stood a little straighter. "I'm sure it's all very fine."

He smiled at her and patted her hand. "I'll bring some more beef, ma'am, and later on we'll get you a little corn mash." He winked and turned to go.

Charlotte Mexia had her own skewered beef. She held it between her thumbs and forefingers, letting the little fingers extend out, with the charm of a fancy lady eating tea cakes. She nibbled at the surface. She nodded, and her eyebrows arched as if to compliment the taste. With very few words the three ladies and the itchy little girl found their space on the ground to eat a precious meal.

The crowd sitting on the ground around the mess camp grew larger. It reminded Elizabeth of the dinner-on-the-ground Sunday meetings at the church her brothers-in-law helped organized. Church lasted all day for those Pilgrim Regular Predestinarian Baptists, with some singing, hours of preaching, maybe some foot-washing and possibly some baptizing. She had worshiped with them back in Illinois and more recently at the Parker place out on the Texas plains.

Those were serious worshipers, those Parkers. Sometimes in the best of weather the worship took place outside. Those men loved outdoors. They loved to hunt, and outside was as much "church" as inside any four walls. She remembered the long prayers that had been offered under cascading trees, and she wondered what the church people had done about Santa Anna.

Just as all this passed through Elizabeth's memory, a man stepped into the crowd and asked them all to bow for prayer. Elizabeth didn't really hear the prayer-words he said. She was too amazed at how it happened. Just as if she had willed it with her memories of worship, the Lord's blessings were being recognized, not just in her private thoughts, but right there, out loud, for everybody to hear. It was true, those in Harrisburg had been blessed with life in spite of the horrors they had known. Elizabeth said a prayer for Sydnie and then focused on the preacher.

As the prayer went on, she listened to the words. "We need Your guidance, Lord. Show us Your way." He said. *Maybe God is in this,* Elizabeth thought. She remembered a verse from Isaiah that mentioned ashes. It promised "beauty for ashes." Could there ever be beauty again in this burned up place? She wanted very much to believe that the Republic of Texas would really be a beautiful thing, rising up from the ashes of the revolution.

When the prayer was over and the "amen" was echoed across the masses, Elizabeth and Charlotte sat with the mother and her child in the crowd eating their beef. And for the space of time it takes to eat a chunk of meat, it seemed to Elizabeth that maybe there was hope for recovery from the brief war, if not the complete fullness of the initial dreams that brought them all to Mexican Tejas. She wondered, *What will happen to us now? Could this land called "TEXAS" really be a new nation? If we couldn't get legal papers before, will we get them now? Who from? Who will be our leader? How will we make a government?*

Her thoughts were interrupted by the arrival of her husband and Tom. Chico brought them to find the women, just as he had promised. "The axel is ready, Mrs. Charlotte. Just like new. This here is a mighty fine wainwright!" Tom gestured toward Benjamin as the two men approached Elizabeth and Mrs. Mexia.

"Chico, go get some of your skin salve," Charlotte said. It was about then that Chico saw the angry fissures of the little girl's arms. She stood up and held out her little arm. She grimaced with the itching, tapping her foot to avoid the scratching.

"Ay, caramba! Sí, señora, yo voy!" he said. His eyes grew wide, and he stood holding the little arm. Then he left in a trot.

Charlotte reassured the little girl, "just a little bit more, Honey. Chico has something that will take the itch right out of that."

Elizabeth was smitten with the compassion of her new friend. They all took their seats on the ground and waited for food and salve.

Charlotte turned to Benjamin. "Mr. Kellogg, it seems you have saved us days of trouble. How can I ever repay you?" Charlotte looked at him expecting him to really tell her what he wanted in payment for fixing the wagon.

Benjamin Kellogg was a man willing to take a good deal when one was offered. He leaned back, raised his eyebrows and thought about what her offer could mean. She was obviously a wealthy woman with resources.

"Well, ma'am, we can sure make a deal," he said smiling, with a hint of seriousness.

Elizabeth overheard and wondered what her husband had in mind.

## Hatching a Plan — Noon May 3rd

"Corn mash is ready, and we got tins, if you want some." It was the man with the rope suspenders. He was carrying more beef chunks, and he handed one each to Tom and Benjamin.

"Thank you, Jack. We'll be there," Tom said. "I'll go," he said to the group. "I'll bring back what I can." He got up and followed the man in rope suspenders.

Charlotte watched Tom leave just as Chico appeared with a tin of salve. He went immediately to the little girl and rubbed the buttery cream onto her arms. The child seemed to melt with the comfort of it. She looked at her mother and smiled. Then Chico turned to the woman. "Y usted?" he motioned that she should also submit to his treatment. She dipped her fingers in the tin and brought a dab of the goo to her neck. "Yes, this is wonderful," she said to him, smiling. He handed her the tin, and she smoothed some onto her shins.

"That is a miracle cure," she said, handing the tin back to Chico. He put his flat hand toward her. "No, señora, es para ustedes." he said. "It is for you."

"Yes, you take it," Charlotte said. "Put it on every day. It will heal you, and you won't itch."

The woman took the tin. "You won't hurt anymore," she said to her daughter. The little girl took a few steps toward Chico and reached up to him. He bent down, closed his eyes and hugged her gently.

"We need to get back to our camp," the woman said. "My people will be worried."

"Of course," Charlotte said. "May God bless you."

That was all. The woman and her daughter left the camp, and the Kelloggs turned their focus onto the business at hand.

"Mr. Kellogg, I insist on paying you for your work," Charlotte said. "Can you give me an idea of what you're owed for your time?"

"Well, Mrs. Mexia, I understand you're headin' northwest, up to that Nashville Colony. Is that right?"

"Yes, I need to get back to our camp out there," she said. "We'll be meeting some people on business, and they're planning on us arriving on time. Looks like we can leave in the morning, thanks to your help."

Benjamin chewed a bit of meat with one eye closed. His thick lips bulged out, and his jaw muscles flexed with each bite, as he thought about his words. He swallowed and cleared his throat. "Well, ma'am . . . seein' as how you and my wife sort of made acquaintance, I thought maybe she might ride along with you a ways. We could call ourselves even by you giv'n her passage up to her family's place."

"Oh, that would be lovely! Where is your family, Elizabeth?"

Elizabeth couldn't reply. She wanted to go visit her family, but Benjamin hadn't discussed the details of how that might happen. "What do you have in mind, Benjamin?" she asked with some confusion.

"Well . . . Tom told me about their place," he said to Elizabeth. Then he turned to Charlotte. "If my calculations are right, 'Lizabeth's people are right on the way. They got a big spread out there. They brought enough people with them to start a whole town of their own. It's out there in that Nashville Colony. I figure . . . you'll go right through their place, and if you don't mind makin' sure she is with her family, then it won't be too much out of your way to just keep on going to your place." He brought his hands down around his knees, held one wrist with the other hand, dangling the beef chunk on its stick in front of him. He looked at Charlotte and then at Elizabeth. "How does that sound to you, 'Lizabeth?"

"And where will you be, Benjamin? How will I find you again?" Elizabeth wanted to know. "Are you going on to Gonzales?"

"Well, no, look around you here." He gestured to the ruins of Harrisburg. "There's work here for any man willing to take it. I figured I can make some money, and we'll have a little grubstake to go back and rebuild in Gonzales. You go and rest. You visit your mama. That will do you a world of good."

They didn't discuss it anymore, but both their hearts were broken over Benjamin's son Johnny who went to the Alamo and didn't come home. Now Johnny's wife, Sydnie was dead. Their baby had gone on to Gonzales with Sydnie's parents, the Davises. The Kelloggs were both due for something good.

"You go and try to recover some, 'Lizabeth. I'll work here, and I'll come find you when the time is right. Then we'll go back to Gonzales together."

Elizabeth was struggling to process the sudden plan. It all sounded too good to be right. Something like this should take more planning and more private talk between a husband and wife. But there wasn't more time for planning. Charlotte was leaving with Tom and Chico the very next morning. She would have to decide.

"That would be wonderful, if it works for you, that is," she said to Charlotte. She waited for Mrs. Mexia to process the possibility.

About that time Tom walked into the conversation with four tin cups of hot corn mash. A lump of tallow butter was melting on the top of each one, and each tin had a stick to serve as a scoop. As he handed them out, Charlotte explained the plan.

Apparently, Mrs. Mexia was more spontaneous than her new friend. "I would love the company, Benjamin." She said as she reached out to take her corn mash. "I'd love to have another woman in my wagon — that would be a nice change, wouldn't it be, Tom?" She embraced the plan immediately.

"Well, now the trip is rugged," Tom warned. "We travel hard when we make this trip. We've never had any *real* trouble, but we never know what will be in our path. If you're up to the trip, you're welcome to come along."

Elizabeth smiled with the thought of it as she quietly swirled the butter into her corn blend. She remembered the prayer for guidance. In a secret place in her heart she confirmed that the hand of God was on them, despite the recent terrors. "I think the trip will be safe," she said. "I think this is a blessing I couldn't have planned better."

Charlotte confirmed the plan with a guarantee of sorts. "We'll look for your people, Elizabeth. We'll try every way to find that camp. But if we have trouble and we can't find them, you can come on with me. Then we can send word to Benjamin so he knows where you are. How does that sound?"

It was the best thing Elizabeth had heard in years. And so it was settled. They agreed to a meeting place for in the morning, and each went their own way for the afternoon.

## Packing to Go — Afternoon May 3rd

After the beef and the corn mash, the Kelloggs retreated to their wagon for the rest of the day, anxious for the trip ahead. Benjamin went to the front end of his wagon and rummaged through the "jockey box." If he was going to hire out, he knew he'd be a more valuable hand with his own tools.

Elizabeth stood by the wagon watching him, admiring his ambition yet regretting their pending separation. She was a willowy figure in a tattered skirt tied tightly at her tiny waist. Her blouse fell a little lower at the neck now, having had the collar torn away weeks ago. It turned in at the waist and continued with a peplum over her narrow hips. The long sleeves were rolled up just below her elbows. Her hands were clasped in front of her.

"I'll sure be missing you, Benjamin." Elizabeth looked at her husband for a precious moment. "I hate to think of going through hard days without you." Knowing Charlotte was without her Anthony made Elizabeth appreciate Benjamin all the more. Benjamin drove, repaired, packed, interceded; Benjamin did it all. Elizabeth never needed a hired guard or a hired driver. She knew no one could take her husband's place.

Benjamin stopped sorting and leaned in toward his wife. "I thought you really wanted to go to your mama's place for a while, Darlin'."

"Yes, I do. I need to. But I'm so tired of the running," she said. She took a few steps and leaned a shoulder against the front rib of the wagon. Then she put her back to the wagon frame and looked longingly into the afternoon sky. "Wouldn't it be wonderful to be settled again, Ben? Wouldn't it be wonderful to just be farmers again? Maybe the Davises would bring the baby to our cabin, and we could just be happy for a while."

Benjamin linked his fingers and put his hands on the box of tools. He dipped his head down between his elbows and imagined the life his wife described. "We'll get back there. The Mexicans will leave us alone now." He lifted his head and looked at his wife. "We'll get back to Gonzales and start again."

Elizabeth looked down, tightened her lips, and nodded her head.

Elizabeth couldn't talk about it. Her adopted son—Benjamin's only child—at age nineteen had gone to the Alamo with the others from Gonzales, expecting to return victorious again, in just a few days. But Santa Anna had killed them all. It wasn't fair.

Elizabeth Duty Kellogg had never had her own children. There had been times she realized it would have been harder to have little ones to suffer in those cruel early Texas days. But she wanted family. She had taken Benjamin's son as her own when she married his father. They had all been close, and when Johnny took Sydnie as his wife, Elizabeth felt the grip of those connections. Anticipating Sydnie's baby had been a sweet thing in Elizabeth's life, only to be soured by Santa Anna's unmerciful interruption.

Now Johnny was gone. Sydnie was gone. The only Kellogg family she had left was Sydnie's baby who went back to Gonzales with George and Rebecca Davis. Elizabeth knew the Davises would welcome them back into the family, and the young child would be a part of their lives, eventually. But first Elizabeth needed a rest, and Benjamin needed to work. Elizabeth would go to her mother's place, and Benjamin would work in Harrisburg for as long as the work lasted. Then they would go back home to Gonzales. They both were realists, and they both believed that was the best plan.

Benjamin helped Elizabeth climb into the wagon, and they each turned to finish their work.

As Elizabeth rearranged and tried to organize the items left in the bottom of the wagon, she spied a bit of calico, a faded green fabric dotted with tiny yellow flowers. It was Sydnie's apron. She tugged on it. The fabric was wrapped around a ladle, which slipped from the cloth and clanked inside a big pot. As she pulled the apron free, the clink of metal coins jangled in the pot.

These were the precious few valuables that survived the recent turmoil in Gonzales. Sydnie and her closest friend Anita had wisely emptied the cash box from Tom Miller's store where they both worked. Then Gonzales was set ablaze. The girls wrapped handfuls of coins in their clothes and brought them along. As the days had gone by, the coins had gotten mixed up with other treasures in both family wagons. Elizabeth rewrapped the coins in the apron and tied that around the handle of the ladle. She secured it in the pot and pushed the pot into the corner of the wagon behind her travel bag.

As Elizabeth pushed, another texture caught her eye. It was faded red, almost pink with age, with a few holes worn here and there. It was John Gaston's wool cap. Sydnie brought it with her. It had belonged to her brother for over ten years. He wore it in Kentucky to ride horses. He wore it as they sailed across the great Gulf from New Orleans. He wore it to every important event until for some reason he didn't wear it to the Alamo. Sydnie took it after she knew he was dead. It was all she had left of him, a symbol of their childhood affection.

"Benjamin," Elizabeth said as she held up the cap for him to see.

"Oh, look at that." He said softly, taking the cap from her. He held it, inspected it slowly. He looked at his wife.

"Can you take me to where she's buried? We can leave it there."

"Yes, she'd like that." He said.

Together the two tired people walked to the community of graves. Elizabeth clutched the cap to her chest and followed her husband along the trail to the bayou. It was early spring, and in spite of the recent rains, in spite of the trampling of war horses, vengeful troops and fire, Mother Nature was showing off her wildflowers.

Benjamin led her to the proper mound of dirt, there amid other graves. There was no need to rush. No one was chasing them now. They just wanted to be quiet. Benjamin put his arm around his wife's narrow shoulders. Her head dropped forward, and she cried. She lifted the cap, and Benjamin took it from her. He bent down and hung it on the cross he had put at one end of the mound. He knelt and touched the ground. Elizabeth put her hand on his shoulder, and they were quiet.

The sun was lower in the sky behind them. The chorus of cicadas and crickets on the wind was a comfort in contrast to the muffled sounds of the camp in the distance.

"Let's go," she said as she tapped his shoulder. He stood, and they walked slowly away from the graves.

## Saying Goodbye — Early Evening May 3rd

Back at their camp the Kelloggs prepared for their imminent separation. Benjamin took Elizabeth's hand. "Come sit with me and let's have ourselves a talk now." He led her to a back wheel of the wagon.

She sat cross-legged, flat on the ground. She reached to the back of her neck and pulled away a large comb that held her bun in place. Her hair loosened. She ran her fingers upward through the strands, scratched her scalp a bit and threaded the hair through her fingers.

In her fortieth year, Elizabeth had a mysterious beauty that defied the hardships of her life. The rugged demands of her escape from Santa Anna had only enhanced her character. Paltry meals, erratic sleep, filth and degradation had worn away her weaknesses and unveiled her strengths. She was firm and graceful, thin and taut, strong in both body and spirit. As he sat in front of her, Benjamin looked at his wife and smiled. She was made for these times. She was tough.

While her tenacity had earned her a stake in Texas, it had marked her in one distinct way. What last year was a dark head of hair was now streaked with white. It brought to Benjamin's mind the black furrowed fields streaked with snow in the winter back in Illinois. He reached out and let his fingers trace a streak that went from her crown, around her ear and down to her neck. Like the snowy fields, her hair still fell in beautiful drifting waves, and he took notice of how beautiful she still was.

He took her hands in his. Those hands were tough enough to skin a fresh-killed rabbit and were tender enough to turn the fragile pages of her bible. They reminded him of the leaves in winter, brown with a deep texture and showing every vein. The scrape to the Sabine had left her lips dry and peeling. But her green eyes, they were forever beautiful and true. Yes, Elizabeth had a rare quality, a ruggedness that got better with age. Benjamin knew she would always be beautiful to him.

She folded her hands in her lap and looked at her husband, quietly waiting for him to speak. This was their last day together for a spell; she didn't know for how long. Whatever he wanted to say now was important to her. "Tell me, now. What is on your mind?" she asked.

Benjamin leaned against the wheel, raised one leg and put that foot down in front of him on the ground. "Now, Elizabeth, the greatest trouble you're going to face on this trip is the possibility of Indians. I don't think you'll be having bandits."

Elizabeth remembered the raids and scalping they had experienced with Indian attacks on Gonzales. There had been plenty. But fortunately for the Kelloggs, they had always gotten away in time.

He paused and looked toward the west. "Lord, anything a bandit wants is right out in the open," he gestured with his hand.

He held both of her hands and tried to feel what she must be feeling. "We've been through a lot, now. I know you're tired." He brushed the hair back from her forehead. "You take a rest, talk to your Mama and your sisters. You see those young ones you missed so much. They'll be growin' so, you won't recognize them!" he forced a laugh.

"This will be a help to us both. I'll miss you too. I really will." He lifted her hand and kissed it sweetly for a long time. He looked out at the fading sun, realizing the afternoon had gone. He spoke in a voice that drifted off into the evening. "We'll be fine, Elizabeth. Just a little more work here, and then we'll go back to Gonzales. And we'll be fine."

"That Mrs. Mexia has made this trip many times," Elizabeth said. Benjamin knew she meant it as a question, wanting him to confirm that her hosts really knew the way to do this right.

"Yes, my love. I believe they have." He leaned his head back, squinting from the sun that sat just on the horizon. "From what Tom said, he has driven this route many a time." He paused and looked at her from the corner of his eye.

"Do you feel good about it? You don't have to go." He turned back to her and waited for her to think about it.

Elizabeth moved over to the wheel and leaned against her husband's shoulder. She looked into the sky, imagining they were all up there together. She remembered John Benjamin Jr., young and strong. She remembered his wife, Sydnie, determined to the end. And she allowed herself one more thought of Sydnie's brother, John Gaston. Such love they all shared in Gonzales, all these young people who were her hope then for *her* family. She knew she needed to completely let them go. That red cap they just left on Sydnie's cross should be her final farewell.

Then she remembered the little boy she wanted to see back in Gonzales, the littlest John Benjamin. He would be her only grandson. And she remembered her own mother who was old. This was a big land. She might not have another chance to travel with another woman in a wagon with a driver and a guard. "I have to go," she said. "It's the right thing to do. It'll do me good."

"Shall we try to get some sleep?" Benjamin leaned forward as he offered his hand.

The couple got up from the ground and climbed into their wagon. The evening grew pleasant. As darkness arrived, the glow of campfires began dotting the town. The rubble disappeared in the darkness, and the peaceful camp offered enough harmony for a good night of much-needed rest.

As they completed their last efforts to prepare for tomorrow's departure, Benjamin continued his assurances while Elizabeth packed her things.

"With homesteads abandoned like they are, bandits can hold up in any place out there," he said. He looked out the back of the wagon across the prairie. "Out there, a man on the run could take whatever he wants without much push-back." He looked at Elizabeth in a serious search of her face. "But the Indians, Elizabeth. Tom told me how they travel to avoid the Indians. They'll run all day tomorrow, run hard. You need to brace for that. This trip won't be easy, but if you can get to the Parker place without Indians, you'll be fine."

Benjamin took hold of the canvas opening in the back of their wagon and remembered his amazement when he first saw the Parker family compound. "The reason they built that place out there was for security from Indians," he said as he squinted his eyes and remembered the extent of care those Parkers had taken in designing the place. Twelve-foot walls with spikes at the top so if anyone managed to scale the fence, they would risk being impaled. There were heavy double gates it took

several men to open. And blockhouses were built so guards could give advance notice in case of a raid. "Nobody's gon'na bother you in there," he said.

As Benjamin crouched in the back of his wagon, he reflected on all he had lost in the last two months. He thought about being without Elizabeth as soon as tomorrow, and he began to feel strangely vulnerable. Slowly he began to think about being alone in Harrisburg and the danger of letting his wife go off with strangers. The night was very still, and an owl hooted in the distance.

## Sharing the Wealth — Evening May 3rd

"Ben, I have something I want to leave with you." Elizabeth kneeled, facing the corner where she had tucked the big cooking pot with the apron full of coins. "I still have these, remember? The girls gave them to us. You take some."

"No, Darlin', you take it. I'll have a job, and they'll feed me. I'll have the wagon. You take it because you might need it," he told her.

"You have to take at least one. Here, take this five-dollar gold piece." She reached out to him with the coin in her hand. "If I know you, you'll probably still have it when we get to Gonzales. But just in case you need it, you'll have it, and I'll be more at peace about you if I know you have some money to get you by in a pinch."

She unfolded the fabric of the apron to reveal the collection of coins. It was a variety of treasures, some coins from Mexico, some from the United States. Some were from the old Spanish days, and there were glass beads the Indians used for barter.

Tom Miller's tavern, the general store and the hotel had been the soul of Gonzales' economy. He accepted cash, promissory notes and anything of value to keep things moving along. Tom sold the store just before he and the other men left for the Alamo. But neither Tom nor the new owner of the store were around to close it down in the Santa Anna panic. What was Anita to do, throw the money in a hole in the ground? That didn't seem right. So she took it.

Anita had hastily handed out the paper money shoving bills and promisories to any women she saw on the street as she made her way to Sydnie's wagon. Those distraught widows probably didn't even know what she gave them, but she hoped they would eventually recognize it, and it would help them.

The coins were tied up in Sydnie's work apron and under 'Nita's skirt. While they were all in Louisiana waiting for word of Sam Houston's victory, the girls divided up the cash. Anita and the Davises took some coins back to Gonzales, and the rest was left with Sydnie.

Benjamin motioned to his wife to come to the back of the wagon where the moonlight was filtering through. His eyes went wide when he saw what she had. He knew there were "coins," but to see them now, to realize the value of it, was overwhelming. For a moment he just quietly looked at the collection of coins glimmering in his wife's hands. Then he took the one she intended for him, a large yellow disc marked "5D." He turned it in his hands. He wasn't thinking so much about its monetary value but more about the journey it had made.

Someone from somewhere had come a long way. They had gone to Gonzales, and with this coin they had purchased something good, maybe a season of rest in Tom's hotel, maybe a good horse and saddle. Maybe this coin had bought a wagon or fed a family on "account" at Tom's store for a season. And then, when Santa Anna forced the destruction of everything precious in town, Anita had the good sense

to save it. In the midst of the chaos, when years of work were being destroyed, this valuable piece was set aside. And now Benjamin was the keeper of the coin. Suddenly he was overcome.

"You know, Elizabeth, this is truly precious," he said. He leaned back against the rib of the wagon, clutching the coin and squeezing his eyes shut. "How simple we are," he said. His voice crackled, and he struggled to get the words out. Elizabeth realized he was uncharacteristically sentimental. She clinched the rest of the coins to her chest, looked at him and waited to hear his thoughts.

"Our homes are gone. Our children are gone," he began to shake as he waved his arms. His face was contorted with his efforts to control his sudden humiliation.

Elizabeth realized she had never seen Benjamin lose control of his emotions. She had always depended on him to be strong, and he always had been. But suddenly he had reached his breaking point, and it was embarrassing.

"Our friends are gone," he continued in between gasps of breath. "Our crops are ruined. Everything we did for years... all a waste of time." He gently pounded his fist against the floor of the wagon and held up his fist holding the coin. "And our hopes are left to a simple piece of metal I can hold in one hand." His voice went high and weak as he let himself sob.

Elizabeth wrapped her arms around him and stroked his curly hair.

Benjamin's only son had been killed at the Alamo just weeks ago. From the moment they learned of it, Benjamin had pushed the fact out of his mind. There were plenty of distractions. The women of Gonzales needed him to be strong, and he was. He packed his family and packed the Alamo widows. He burned his home, drove his oxen, buried babies, fought off prairie outlaws, and summoned up the tenacity to get the whole town across the Sabine. Even in Louisiana, he comforted where comfort was needed. But he had never mourned his own son.

But now, having buried Sydnie and preparing to say goodbye to Elizabeth, he had reached his limit. He needed to grieve.

"Benjamin, you're such a good man," Elizabeth told him. "You've given everything you had in you."

Through his tear-filled eyes Benjamin looked at her. "Is it enough?" he asked in a very quiet and sincere voice. "Do I have enough left? Do I still have what it takes to start all over again?"

"Oh, yes, Benjamin. If anybody has what it takes, you do," she told him. "Just think of it. You're doing the work of all three men who help Mrs. Mexia," she pointed out with sincere admiration.

He wiped his face on his shirt sleeve and sniffed.

She hugged him. "Our only hope for life out here is left to men like you, Ben, men who are willing to work in a mess like Harrisburg and build it all over again. If this is what you want, we can start again," she assured him.

"Well, Darlin', this coin is going to be my inspiration. I will have it when I get back to Gonzales. I'll look at it and remember where it came from, what it went through and the people who brought it this far." He looked intently at Elizabeth, and for a moment they were both quiet.

"I'm gonna go get some air, and I'll be back," he said as he crawled out the back of the wagon.

## Hiding the Coins — Night May 3rd

Elizabeth knew Benjamin needed to regain his composure. He was not given to emotion, and grieving his son was a painful experience for him.

While he was gone, she hatched an idea for hiding the coins. She pulled up the skirt of her dress and exposed the cotton slip she wore underneath. She pulled the thread that held the hem in place and made an opening. She took a few of the half-dimes and let them trickle into the wide hem of her underskirt. She manipulated them to the right side, and then toward the back, far away from the little hole she made. *They'll stay back there*, she thought.

Then she tore the left side seam, exposing the raw edge. She pulled the frayed fabric into a longish tail. She took several quarter-eagles, twisted the fabric into a little pocket and tied them securely. There were two more gold quarters, so she did the same little tear and pocket on the front of her underskirt.

Benjamin returned just as she was finishing the scheme. "What 'cha doin', Darlin'?"

"I'm taking the rest of this money to Mama's with me," she said as she showed him what she had done. "See here, how I hid it?" She pulled the underskirt around and showed him the little pockets she made.

"You're just that clever," he said in admiration.

"I don't know what I'll do with it, but you'll know I have it. I promise to keep as much as I can, and when we get back to Gonzales, we'll both have something to lean on for starting all over then." She re-wrapped the remaining coins in Sydnie's apron and tied it all in the smallest, tightest little bundle she could make and shoved it into her travel bag.

Elizabeth and Benjamin spread their blankets on the floor of their little wagon. Tomorrow would be the beginning of another separation they believed would be brief. Neither of them could know this would be their last night together.

# Part Two:
# Journey to Family

## Off to San Felipe — Morning May 4th

"Good morning, Benjamin." Charlotte Mexia and her two hired men were standing at their camp when the Kelloggs walked up. Tom was wearing a fresh bib shirt with the sleeves rolled up off his wrists. His face was scrubbed clean.

"Mornin', ma'am, Tom, Chico." Benjamin said as he put Elizabeth's little travel bag into the back of the Mexia wagon.

Benjamin turned to Tom with a serious look on his face. "Tom, I'm countin' on you to take care of her, now."

"You can do that, Ben. I 'spec we'll meet again one day, and I'll not be shaming myself," Tom laughed. "I'll be sure your missus is safe. If we can't leave her off with her family, we'll take her on with us. I'll bring word back here to you. We'll be back through here before winter. Mr. Anthony has a lot of work down there in Galveston and New Orleans. He keeps us on the move that way." Tom nodded his head with confidence, and Benjamin felt the assurance of it.

Elizabeth stood by her husband as they both heard the promises Tom made. Then Benjamin bent down to her, and she stretched high to hug his neck. They shared a long, lingering embrace. She wanted to remember the smell of his skin in the days ahead, to take at least that much with her. "I love you," she whispered in his ear.

"I'll see you soon," he said. "You try to rest for a bit."

She let him go and touched his cheek. "I'll be expecting to see that coin," she teased him as she felt the betrayal of a tear slipping out of her eye. She sniffed the sadness away and stepped up to the Mexia wagon.

Chico came around then, with his sombrero rolled in his hand and the jangle on his boot. He looked excited about the impending journey. Elizabeth recalled the excitement in young Johnny's face every time he left on his adventures, remembering the time he didn't come home. There was no assurance anywhere in this country. Every journey was a gamble. But without the gamble, there could be no fulfillment of their hopes for a peaceful farming life on their very own spread out in Texas.

Tom hitched up four strong, young mules to the Conestoga. Charlotte and Elizabeth settled inside under the canvas bonnet, and Chico mounted a well-mannered mare. Once again, a wagon full of hopeful pioneers rolled out in search of the Promised Land.

## A Highway Bandit — Midday May 5th

The Mexia's Conestoga was the best wagon Elizabeth had ever seen. The heavy canvas looked new, and the ribs that supported it were double thick, compared to those on Ben's Prairie Schooner. The wheels ran smooth, and the feel of it was solid and sure. The team was fresh, four young mules with all the eagerness of youth.

"We'll make long days of it," Charlotte began to explain to Elizabeth. "Tom will drive each day until he can't see any more. We'll go to San Felipe first, probably get there the third night. Then the next morning we'll head north along the Brazos. When the Brazos meets the Navasota, we'll stop again at a little place called Washington. It'll be at least several weeks on the trail, full days of hard road. But we've never had any real trouble."

"Try to make yourself comfortable. We'll need to move about as best we can. I get so stiff on these runs," Charlotte said as she stretched her legs out a bit.

The Conestoga was the roomiest space Elizabeth had ever travelled in. She stretched her legs and arms out to get a feel for it. Then she reached to the back of her neck and repositioned the comb she depended on to keep her bun in place.

Charlotte opened the back of the canvas. "I like to see where we've been," she said. "Come look out with me."

Elizabeth crawled into place, and the two women sat on opposite sides, looking out the back of the wagon. Harrisburg was shrinking in the distance. The terrain was flat prairie with clumps of trees. Everything was an impressive green, after the brown of a charred town, and the depressing dreariness of their flight to Louisiana. Elizabeth delighted in the new growth she saw in the woods. As she and Charlotte sat quietly watching, a swirl of wind was cast up behind the wagon. The whirlwind grew, and then it spun off to the east.

Elizabeth closed her eyes and remembered a whirlwind she read about in her Bible. It was part of the plight of a man who had suffered great losses, just like the Texas pioneers had suffered. A man named Job had been plagued with destruction of his property, the death of his children and ridicule by his closest friends. But in the end, he had recovered. The story said he gained twice his original wealth in the end. Elizabeth wanted to believe that story was meant for the people of Gonzales. For a brief moment she tried to imagine how the little town would look years from now, rebuilt and prospering. She imagined seeing her grandson looking up at her with his daddy's smile. But for now she needed to see her mama and her sisters.

Charlotte interrupted Elizabeth's thoughts. "How did you come to be in Harrisburg?" she asked.

With her typical reservations, Elizabeth locked eyes with Charlotte and thought about how she might best explain it. She nodded her head and held up one finger as if to say, "hold on, and I'll tell you . . ." Charlotte already knew Elizabeth well enough to understand this gesture, and she gave Elizabeth all the time she needed to think about what she would say.

"It was that San-Tanna," she started. "We were living in Gonzales, and all our young men went to San-Antone to fight him." She paused in her story. It was painful to put it into words. Charlotte nodded and pulled at a strand of black hair that had blown out of place.

Elizabeth looked out into the prairie behind them, watching the past fade away; the sad experiences were disappearing minute by minute in the swirl of dust. "We had a son. We called him John." She smiled, remembering him.

Charlotte nodded and waited, thinking about her own children.

"He went to fight San-Tanna. But he didn't come home. None of them did." She looked out again, remembering the last days of Gonzales and the chaos. She thought about the precious coins and reached around to feel them in the hem of her underskirt.

Charlotte felt the resurrection of her own postponed grief. She still had two young children, but she had shelved away the pain from the loss of her eldest son, Adolfo. She could understand Elizabeth's struggle to explain it.

Then Elizabeth went on with her story. "Well, we got word he was coming. San-Tanna was heading for Gonzales. John had a young wife, and she was expecting their baby, just any day. We had to go, all of us, the whole town. And Lord, the whole world took up with us on the way. We went to the Sabine until we got word to go back home. But Sydnie—after the baby came—she was too sick to go back. They told us Harrisburg was the best place for help, but they didn't know it was burned up. That's where she died."

"And that's who Benjamin was burying when you were sitting on the bench?" Charlotte asked.

Elizabeth just nodded her head and looked down the road behind them.

"My Benjamin was one of the few men who didn't go to San-Antone. He and George Davis, Sydnie's father—those two and about four others were the only men left in Gonzales. Lord, they worked gettin' us all out of there."

Charlotte was privately sympathizing with her friend. They not only shared the loss of a son, but Charlotte also had her own history with the man Elizabeth called "San-Tanna." General Santa Anna was an old acquaintance of the Mexia family but certainly no longer a friend. The Mexia land—the place they were now headed—was selected because it was faraway. It was the retreat Jose Antonio Mexia had chosen for the purpose of keeping his family away from Santa Anna.

Mexia was thought to have betrayed Santa Anna. He was one of the most visionary men in North America, and he had played a political hand against Santa Anna when the general declared himself "President" of Mexico. Santa Anna assumed a dictatorship in his country, and Mexia objected. For that, Jose Antonio Mexia had been exiled from Mexico.

Señor Mexia was a brilliant man. He had formed partnerships outside of Mexico with men who knew shipping, and he had connections all over the world. He spent most of his time away from home, in New Orleans, Cuba or Nicaragua, but those were business trips. In his heart he was a proud Tejano hiding in plain sight out in the plains. He had helped organize a conglomerate that would last for years even beyond Mexia's own life. But in 1836 that company was only a steppingstone in a long path of adventures, both political and personal.

As it happened, Mexia's land interest was just a few miles north of the fortress Elizabeth's family had built, in a colony some men from Nashville, Tennessee were organizing. Since his work took him away from home, it was fortunate that Charlotte was independent, adventurous and confident. In fact, she was more involved in Mexico's business and Mexia's business than most women of those days. With Tom and Chico, she could travel where she wanted. She shared her time between Mexico City, Galveston, New Orleans and Tejas, any place she was needed. She divided her time with her husband and her children and gave support to many causes.

These two women had more in common than they could have known, back there sitting on the bench in Harrisburg. Charlotte's heart warmed to Elizabeth's story, and she wondered how she could explain her own connection to Santa Anna. But that would have to wait.

"Whoa! Hold up there!" Tom shouted and the wagon came to an abrupt halt. There was a racket outside, and the sudden jolt threw the women off balance. Elizabeth started toward the back opening, but Charlotte signaled her to stay back. Charlotte put her fingers to her lips. "Shhh," she warned. Then her mouth formed the words, "be quiet." They listened.

"What's in the wagon?" a man's voice asked.

Tom put him off. "Got nothin' in here you'd want. Just trying to get back home is all."

Charlotte reached into the pocket of her leather skirt and drew out a shiny derringer. She held it to her side and cocked it.

"Where's home?" The highwayman asked.

"Up the Navasoot," Tom said. "We're headed for San Felipe and then we'll go north, up the Brazos. Got no business here, just passing along the road."

The man led his horse slowly around the wagon, and then the leather moaned as he got off his saddle. Tom was getting irritated. "Got no time to sit and jaw, now. We've got a long way to go."

"Well, you're crossin' my land. And I figure maybe a bounty might be proper. I'll just look in the back to see maybe something we can agree on for the privilege of using my road." The man's footsteps made a crunching sound on the ground as he walked toward the back of the wagon.

Charlotte's eyes narrowed into black slits as she lifted the little derringer toward the back opening of the wagon canvas, aiming it high. As a hand reached into the opening Charlotte pulled the trigger. The blast rang out and reverberated in the enclosure. The hand disappeared and the wagon jolted forward. Tom and Chico yelled out their commands as the mules bolted. Elizabeth closed her eyes as she tumbled over.

When she was recovered and could sit up again, Elizabeth asked, "Did you kill him?"

Charlotte laughed, "Oh, no, I would never do that. I could hear his boots. He was walking. I knew he'd be standing low to the wagon. So I aimed my shot high, just to scare him off. The sound is always worse inside this thing. This isn't the first time we've had encounters like this. We don't even have to think about it anymore. Tom and Chico know I'm ready. We just get rid of 'em and go on our way."

Elizabeth's new friend was of one of the ablest women in North America. Their fortuitous acquaintance would accomplish what otherwise might have been near impossible at that time, to get Elizabeth back to her mother. Tom and Chico drove the wagon into the night without any more interruptions.

## San Felipe — Midnight May 6th

For three days the strong, young mules slogged west through the rain and mud. On the third day they pushed on to finally reach San Felipe. They arrived at midnight. Glad at last to make camp, Tom tended the mules while Chico made a fire. Somehow, throughout the journey he always had food cooking by the time the women finished laying out their bedding.

Charlotte and Elizabeth stood looking down the main street of the heart of Austin's colony. The moon was new that night, offering no light at all. A heavy cloud cover only deepened the blanket of darkness around them. In contrast the campfires distinguished the place like happy little candles across the town, celebrating the progress of the Mexia wagon.

San Felipe had been plundered, just like Harrisburg, but the rubble was hidden in the dark. Elizabeth suspected as much and was glad not to see it.

"You be careful," Tom warned as Charlotte and Elizabeth carefully crept around in the dark unpacking for the night.

Elizabeth tossed bundles of bedding out from the back of the wagon. "This was Mr. Austin's home," Elizabeth said thoughtfully. "I wonder where he is tonight."

"He's a good man, that Austin," Charlotte remembered. "Do you know him?"

Elizabeth hopped down from the wagon, and Charlotte helped her unroll the blankets.

"He was known in our parts. I never met him, but I reckon he'll be around now to make the new government," Elizabeth said.

Elizabeth tried to sort out in her mind how a government was made from scratch. She contemplated how new villages would be resurrected from the ashes of burned-out towns and how food would be salvaged from the ruined crops left trampled by the Mexican horses. They had all been through this before. Would enough people come back and try again?

Chico drummed a big wooden spoon on the coffee pot to get their attention. "Come eat!" he called to them.

The four travelers gathered near the wagon where Chico was cooking. The glow of the campfire exaggerated Chico's grin. Elizabeth thought how proud he always seemed. She thought he was a good reminder of gratitude, and she was glad for their chance encounter.

Chico presented a skillet of pemmican, lumps of buffalo meat, chopped and dried. The meat was then rolled with other delicacies of the day, brown beans, some corn meal, all mushed together with hog fat. All that had been done weeks ago back in Mexico. Fat little meat biscuits were dried in the sun and packed into straw baskets lined with sail cloth.

Chico carefully inventoried his supplies daily. Anthony Mexia might be miles and miles away from his family, but he made sure Tom, Chico and Charlotte had what they needed. Back in Mexico Chico had a wealth of supplies—pots, pans, baskets, sail cloth, spices, tools of all kinds, things from all over the world Anthony brought to his family. Chico didn't have to resort to "salvage." He had the best and the newest, and he used it all well to fulfill his responsibilities.

In the daylight he might have added some edible vegetation to his meal, something he spied along the trail. But this night was too black, and it was too late to bother. Tonight, he simply cut slices of smoked bacon from the slab he kept in canvas, wrapped them around the meat biscuits and grilled it all in the skillet. Chico knew his way around a campfire, and everyone who travelled with him was glad.

The smell was wonderful, but the meat biscuits were too hot to hold. Tom reached for one and quickly shook his fingers away, cursing. Chico laughed and said something in Spanish Elizabeth didn't understand. Chico took a sharp stick and stabbed one of the lumps from the skillet. He presented it to Tom as if it was a trophy. Tom and Chico had a good-natured exchange of unintelligible words, and they both laughed again. Then Chico presented a stabbed lump to each of the ladies.

They ate their fill of pemmican lumps and washed them down with pulque, a diluted alcoholic beverage Chico made with Mexican agave.

The drink was another of Chico's concoctions from weeks ago. The mixture was mostly water, and the fermented agave ensured it was pure to drink.

For centuries pulque had been a staple for the people of Mexico. Even the children drank it daily. It was made from the plentiful agave plant, and families depended on it as a health potion.

Chico's pulque water delivered energy, nourishment and hydration. Additionally, it had a slight kick, barely detectible, but it helped a person to sleep. When Charlotte was in Mexico City, Chico used his time to prepare such things as pemmican and pulque. He always knew Charlotte would soon take another journey to somewhere. He kept a small wooden barrel of the pulque on the Conestoga, ready for just such a night as this.

Using a dipper, he filled a small jug, which the four travelers shared. Elizabeth wasn't accustomed to the alcohol, but she didn't object. After all, this was an adventure, and she was their guest.

During the meal they heard repeated howls of a coyote. It sounded far away, but Elizabeth noticed that Chico and Tom looked at each other every time they heard it.

After the meal Tom and Chico got up, moved toward the wagon and had a quiet conversation.

"I'll just take a little look-see," Tom said to the women. "I'm sure there ain't nothin' here gonna bother us, but I'll sleep better if I know what's around us here," he said as he checked his rifle. "Chico, we'll be headin' out early," he said as he walked out of their camp.

"Sí, Mr. Tom. I get it all ready," Chico said as he began to clean up.

"Should we do something to help?" Elizabeth asked Charlotte.

"No, dear. Chico wants to take care of his things just the way he likes them. Let's try to sleep," Charlotte said as she led Elizabeth back to their sleeping pallets. "Morning will come, and we'll be exhausted."

Charlotte took the pins out of her hair and clipped them to the edge of her blanket. She shook her head, letting her black mane loose around her shoulders. They each snuggled down into their bedding on the ground.

Charlotte went to sleep almost immediately, but Elizabeth struggled with sleep. Against the black canvas of night, her memory painted ugly pictures of the recent past. She knew what desperation looked like, and she'd had her fill of it. But Elizabeth was not one to hold onto grief. She forced her thoughts to the mysteries of her hosts.

## Stung by a Scorpion — Night May 6th

Elizabeth had always taken pride in her ability to take care of herself. What she thought of as "self-reliance" others may have seen as simple-mindedness. She liked to be quiet, withdrawn and retracted. She didn't involve herself in other people's business, and she didn't allow others to be involved in hers.

Elizabeth thought it was ironic that Charlotte, who was an obviously well-to-do woman, approached Elizabeth, a stranger with little to offer, asking to share a bench back there in Harrisburg. Charlotte's friendship enhanced Elizabeth's sense of herself. She had always been a quiet woman, subdued and unassuming, almost invisible. Could it be that Charlotte truly considered her, "Simple Elizabeth," someone of importance? She wondered who these people really were with whom she travelled and ate and slept?

She turned onto her side and looked at the dying embers of the fire. Chico was sitting there, taking off his boots. He held the left one and contemplated the spur. It seemed that he was having a conversation with it, his lips moving ever so slightly.

As she contemplated the curiosity of it all something large and creepy tickled across Elizabeth's arm. A spider, no doubt.

Elizabeth flung the insect away, but it was too late. She felt an electric burn stab into the muscle of her right forearm. The night was too black to see even near her, so she pulled her blankets over her head and tried to sleep. But sleep wouldn't come.

Her arm began to itch and ache. With her left hand she felt the flesh rise, and the skin was turning hot. Elizabeth sat up, cautiously so as not to disturb Charlotte. She wanted to examine her arm, but the night was too dark.

Tom returned to the camp. He sat on a large stone and began stoking the fire. He kicked out a leg and reached into his pants pocket, drawing out a tobacco pouch. From his shirt pocket he pulled a tiny wad. Carefully he flicked a finger on his tongue and peeled off a thin paper from the wad, shoving the rest of it back into his shirt. With precision he tapped some tobacco into the paper and rolled it.

Keeping his eye on the newly rolled cigarette, he put the bag of tobacco back into his pants. One of the poker-sticks from their supper was lying on the ground close at hand. Tom put the end of the little stick into the campfire until a prominent new flame was born. He let the cigarette and the lighted stick meet very near his lips. Then he smiled a bit and closed his eyes as he took the first draw.

Elizabeth got up and approached the fire. She was beginning to fret over the increasing pain on her forearm. She wanted a better look but didn't want to call unnecessary attention to herself.

As was his nature, Chico noticed her. He approached her but respectfully kept his distance. "Qué pasa, señora?" he asked. "What is wrong?" His thick brows wrinkled over his sad brown eyes, and his mouth turned down with concern. He wondered what could be keeping her from her sleep.

Elizabeth was holding her right forearm with the left hand. When the glow from the fire shone on her Chico could see the swelling. "Ay, señora! Mira tu brazo! Mira, señor Tom!" Chico called to Tom to alert him to Elizabeth's arm.

Tom got up and came to Elizabeth. "You been bit?" he asked with half-parted lips holding onto the cigarette. Elizabeth held out her arm so he could see. "Come over here in the light, ma'am," he told her as he took the cigarette in his fingers.

"Yep, I'd say it got you." Tom looked around. "Too dark to tell what it might be. Did you see it?"

49

"No," she said. "I thought it was a spider, but it felt larger. I flung it away."

"Probably nothing deadly. May be painful a while," Tom said as he turned her arm a bit to get the best view.

By that time Chico brought an onion from his stash of supplies. He cut off a round slice and demonstrated on his own arm that Elizabeth should hold it on the wound. She wasn't sure and looked at Tom for confirmation.

"Yes'm, that'll take the burn right out," he said kindly.

Chico held out the slice. She took it and applied it to her arm. "I'll have to sit up for a while," she said. "If I lay down the onion will fall off."

"No," Chico said as he dashed back to the wagon. In a flash he was back with a large handkerchief. He showed her how he could tie it on to hold the onion. He smiled and wrapped the cloth around his own arm to demonstrate how he intended to help her, waiting for her approval.

She nodded her acceptance. He rolled the sleeve of her blouse down her arm, holding the onion slice in place. Then he tied his bandana over the place, securing the vegetable.

"Una escorpión!" he told her. "A scorpion!" Elizabeth thought he was probably right, considering the size of the insect she felt.

After he completed his task, he patted her arm and gestured toward her bedding. "Para que duermas," he said. "For you to sleep."

"He wants you to be able to sleep," Tom told her.

Elizabeth crawled back into her bedding and pulled her head back under the cover. The fortunate effect of the pulque at supper influenced her just enough so that in spite of the smell of the onion she fell asleep.

## Dreams and Snakes — Morning May 7th

"RUN! RUN!" A child was screaming, chasing her pet goose. "Bring Lollie! I don't want her to burn up," the child cried to her brother. Ducks were squawking and flittering in front of a little boy, trying to help his sister corral the birds. Through the black silhouettes of trees Elizabeth saw flames consuming a row of cottages. She smelled the smoke and realized she couldn't breathe. She tried to run, but she was caught. Her captor shook her violently. With a great thrust she tried to pull away, and then her blanket fell away from her head. She gasped and sat up. She had been dreaming.

"Oh, my!" Elizabeth panted. "What a nightmare!"

"You were screaming and growling and kicking, but I couldn't get to you with your head wrapped in the blanket," Charlotte told her. "I hope I didn't make it worse by shaking you. I wanted to wake you."

Elizabeth looked around. "I was back in Gonzales," she explained. She buried her face in her fists and rubbed her eyes hard. "But now I see we're here, so let's think about today." She pulled her hands away from her face and forced a smile.

"Come on, let's see about some coffee," Charlotte offered her friend a hand and helped Elizabeth stand up. Elizabeth stretched and bent and adjusted her clothes while Charlotte pinned her hair up in back.

"What is that smell?" Charlotte said sniffing the air in the direction of the campfire. "Is Chico cutting onions for breakfast?"

Elizabeth remembered the treatment for her sting. "Look here," she said, taking off the handkerchief and rolling up her sleeve. "I had a bad sting last night, and Chico put this onion chunk on there. Look! The swelling has gone down!"

Charlotte looked at the place where Elizabeth pointed. She wrinkled her nose, twisted her lips, and waggled her hand in front of her face to wave away the odor.

"Leave it to Chico," she said. "If there is a remedy, he'll know it!" She nodded and pointed the way to the campfire as Elizabeth threw the chunk of onion into the grass.

The entire party had slept late on the fourth morning. They were exhausted and didn't get bedded down until the wee morning hours. As they got themselves together to face the day ahead, Chico started stoking up the coffee and browning some corn tortillas in the supper skillet. Charlotte poured two tins of coffee and asked Tom, "How much farther?" She passed a tin to Elizabeth and they sat.

"We'll follow this river home, ma'am. "Lot depends on the troubles we find. Use-to it was a fairly clear path. Lots of folks going this way, for the water and to get bearings by way of the river. But if a tree fell up ahead, or we meet up with another highway robber . . . ." He rubbed his unshaved jaw and propped his foot on the center pin of the back wheel. "Maybe four more days to Washington, ma'am."

Suddenly Chico jumped away from his cooking. He bent his knees in a half-squat and put his arms out to his sides. He was holding a huge fork which looked like a spear in his hand. His behavior scared the wits out of Elizabeth, and everyone went quiet.

They all heard a distinct rattle coming from a canvas bag Chico had thrown aside. The cooking tools travelled in the bag, and it had been on the ground all night. Chico motioned to the women to move, and they quietly slipped away. Chico jabbed his long fork into the canvas and flipped it aside. He leaped to the spot and in minutes produced the remains of a timber rattler. With a grin on his face he pranced toward the fire. "Let's have a bit more breakfast," he said as he tossed it into the skillet.

Elizabeth was learning about her hosts. They were experienced and skilled in all the ways that were needed on the prairie. She felt a deep appreciation for the little man with the jangle in his step, and she realized she was giggling. It had been a long time since Elizabeth had giggled. Benjamin was right. This trip to find her family was good for her.

## Washington, Texas — Morning May 11th

Tchur! Tchur! Knock-knock-knock-knock-d-d-d-d-d-d-d-d....

A woodpecker was the loudest sound in the woods around Washington, Texas as the Mexia wagon rolled along slowly and came to an easy stop. The little village was unoccupied, except for the wildlife. It was the quietest place Elizabeth had ever been. No one said a word. Charlotte and Elizabeth looked at each other and then looked out the back of the wagon.

Respecting the solitude, Charlotte quietly motioned toward the opening. She crawled out, and Elizabeth followed.

In the early spring this part of Texas was bursting into bloom. Under the canopy of ancient oaks, a huge flowering dogwood tree stood in all its glory with its fat white four-platter flowers crowding the graceful branches. A red honeysuckle dangled her petals on a bush nearby, spilling out their perfume.

Elizabeth walked a few yards toward the hardwoods and picked up an acorn so big it filled her hand. She held it up and showed it to Charlotte who nodded her mutual admiration. The place was the soul of peace. It was a sanctuary of nature's quiet beauty. The community structures stood undisturbed. But the people were gone.

The foursome from the Mexia wagon were raptured by the stillness. In contrast to all the chaos they had seen they all just looked around and took in the calm.

Tom broke the silence. "They didn't come here," he said softly.

"No," Charlotte replied. "They left it alone. Isn't it beautiful?"

A square cottage sat predominantly near a grove of oaks. Charlotte pointed to it and walked in that direction.

The cottage was a structure of raw, unfinished timber. The windows were covered with a thin canvas, now frayed and ragged from the recent rainstorms railing against them. There was no door. Charlotte easily stepped inside.

A small table sat center of the single room. Chairs of every description filled the rest of the space. There were chairs stacked in other chairs, chairs against the wall, chairs pushed up to the table, chairs touching chairs all around the room, and even a chair sitting on the table. The place looked like a storehouse for chairs.

"Who put all these chairs in here, and why?" Charlotte asked as she wrapped her fingers around the curved wood of a chair-back.

Tom was moving chairs so he could get to the table. He took the single chair down from the tabletop. He looked around and under the table. "Look," he said, as he brought up a wire bin filled with crumpled paper. "This is the place," he said.

"What place?" Elizabeth asked.

"This is the place where they met to make the rules," he said. "Look here. An ink well." He lifted a tiny glass bowl with a bit of dried black substance inside. "And there are quills all over the floor," he pointed out.

He took a wad of paper out of the wire basket, uncrumpled it, placed

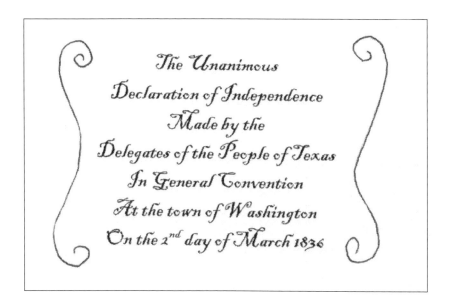

it flat on the table and smoothed it as much as it would smooth. He leaned over, put both hands on the table and studied the paper.

"Yep, look at this," he said holding it up. "These are drafts of the declarations and rules they wanted to make." He held the paper so the light from the door shone on it. "Somebody wrote here about what he declared . . . and then he marked it out. And over here, they were trying to spell something. They tried m-e-r . . . and m-a-r . . . and m-u-r . . . then they marked that all out." He looked at several crumpled papers. "They're all like that. This is their wastepaper from the meeting in here." Tom put the papers down and looked around. "This is the place alright."

Just as Tom put the basket down there was a rustle outside the window. Someone was crouching down outside the window opening. Only the top of a head was visible as it passed by. It was a head of very black hair.

### The Johnson Family — Late Morning May 11th

"You folks live around here?" A bone-thin man with black hair spoke from the doorway of the cottage.

Charlotte spoke up, "No, we're just passing through on our way up the river. My name is Mexia. What's yours?"

"Jordan Johnson," he said. The man swayed and leaned against the doorway, struggling to breathe.

"You hurt?" Tom asked him.

"No, not hurt, just tired and hungry," he said. "Me and my family, we live just up the road a ways at Independence." He gestured out the door. "My wife and boys are out there waiting to see if I can find something for us to eat. We heard the Mexicans were coming, but they never came yet."

Chico excused himself and went outside.

"Where is everybody from town?" Tom asked.

"They all left for fear of the Mexicans, I guess," the man said, watching Chico as he passed him in the doorway. "I was thinking you folks were Indians or Mexicans," Mr. Johnson said.

"No, we just stopped to rest," Tom said. "Haven't you heard about the liberation?"

"No, we ain't heard nothin." He said. "After that meetin' the Washington people came up our way. They came through to get the farmers from Independence, and then they all went east. My wife was sick, so we just stayed back. My place is sort of hidden in the trees, and I just figured we'd ride it out."

Charlotte held up the frayed window canvas to look outside.

Tom pulled out a chair. "Come in here and sit down then," Tom said as he began to explain the news of Texas' victory.

"Back some weeks, they had the last of it," Tom explained. "Out in the field. The Mexican Army was having their siesta, and Sam Houston went in there and took 'em. Didn't last no time. That Santa Anna is on his way to jail, and this here is called 'The Republic' now."

Mr. Johnson sat wide-eyed. "Well, I'll be dern," he said softly and let himself think about all that for a minute.

"I don't see your wagon," Charlotte said.

"No wagon. No horses. Just us." He tried to smile as he took a seat.

"We got spared by the Mexicans, but them Indians, they still raid us. Just yesterday morning early, they came through there and stole our horses. I had a fat sow, and they filled her full of arrows, cut her up and carried her off." He twisted his mouth, shook his head and made a little smacking noise.

"We just climbed down under the hay in the barn and they never knew we were there," Johnson continued. "I guess they figured everybody was gone. They sacked the house and took all the supplies we had. So we dodged the spear this time. But my wife and my boys, we wanted to come see if we could stay over here with the Washington folks for a few days." He coughed, took his handkerchief and wiped the back of his neck. "I guess they're not back yet. No tellin' what's gonna happen next, with this 'Republic' you talkin' about."

Charlotte, Elizabeth and Tom looked at each other and let the man talk.

"We wanted to come here 'cause this is supposed to be an important place, and we figured there'd be protection over here. Don't look so important today." Johnson laughed, pushed his chair back and pushed his fingers into his waist band.

Charlotte nodded to Elizabeth. "I'm going to look into those other cabins," she said. "If there's food in there, you can surely have it. No sense it going to waste." She and Elizabeth walked out the doorway.

"You didn't see anybody else in any of those other cabins you came by?" Tom asked.

"No, sir, didn't see a soul. They had that big meeting here, you know," he said as he gestured across the room. "This was where they wrote all those papers to Mexico, talkin' about independence. They were all here, Old Sam Houston and Austin and Burnet and all of 'em. This place was packed. Then somebody said the Mexican Army was comin', and they flew out of here like a covey."

"That explains all the chairs," Tom said.

In no time at all Elizabeth and Charlotte were back with an arm load of food, two big lumps of bread, some pears, potatoes and an onion. They laid the load on the table.

About that time Chico came back into the hut. "Familia," he said. A woman and twin boys came in behind him. The woman was small. Her boys towered over her, as tall as their father. It was clear they were workers, judging from the muscle in their arms. But it was also clear they weren't fully grown, judging from the peach fuzz on their upper lips.

The boys were amazing mirror reflections of each other. Thick curly hair the color of sand. Their eyes were brown buttons peering out from thick blond lashes. Their only distinguishing marks were the dimples that pulled in when they smiled. One had a deep hollow in his cheek while the other was marked with the same endearing pit in his chin. They stood reverently with their hands behind their back, glancing around the room.

The woman was anxious, noticing the bread on the table. "Oh, Jordan, look at that," she said, glancing at Charlotte. "Can my boys have some, please?"

"Yes, ma'am, these women found all this in those cabins. Come on over here, boys, and have a bite," Tom said.

The woman took one of the loaves and broke it in half, giving a chunk to each of her boys. She split the other loaf and gave half to her husband, taking a quarter of the loaf for herself.

Chico pulled a chair up to the table so the woman could sit with her husband.

"What will you folks do now?" Tom asked.

"I think I'd feel safer staying here until some of the Washington people get back," Johnson said. "My boys been without water since yesterday. I was afraid they poisoned the well, and we need to try the river."

Tom winked at Chico. "We got something better than that," he said. Chico grinned and stepped out the door.

"Ma'am, are you well?" Charlotte asked Mrs. Johnson.

"Yes, I'm fine. We've all been sick with our breathing, but I'm much better now," she said as she took another bite of the bread. "We were all down when the word came about the Mexicans, but we just couldn't go. Our place is well hidden. Jordan built us a fine barn, and we can hide in there so nobody would even notice. We've been out here a little over a year, and we've been able to fend off trouble every time, so far."

Just then Chico came in wearing a proud grin and carrying his jug of pulque. He held it up high and looked at Tom.

"Try some of this," Tom said. Chico handed the jug to Mr. Johnson. He closed one eye and looked into the jug with the other. He gave it a swirl and sniffed it. "What is this stuff?"

"That's the best-preserved water you'll ever find," Tom said laughing. The man frowned and cocked his head suspiciously.

"Honestly," Charlotte said. "It's the way we stay healthy. That's Chico's special water he purifies so we can always keep it in the wagon." She looked at the twin boys. "My children drink it, and they are little ones."

The man took a swig of the liquid and wiped his mouth. "I see what you mean," he said. "I can see where that would keep a person going in a bad time. Here, Mother. You try some."

Mrs. Johnson took a delicate sip as her husband held the jug. "Oh, my. That is something! A bit of a strong tinge, but not so much that a person could really tell it." She looked again at Charlotte. "You say your young ones drink that?" She looked at her boys.

Mr. Johnson spoke up. "Mary, these boys will be learning to drink hooch someday, and that is a good way to start. It's mighty light, and they're here with us. Let them have some. They're thirsty. Aren't you, boys, aren't you thirsty?"

"Yes, Daddy, I am." Chin-dimple reached for the jug, and his father let him take it. The boy drank down several swallows. He wiped his lips with his hand, grinned and passed the jug to his brother.

Everyone watched as the boys drank a few more swallows each. They were both proud and embarrassed, all at the same time, proud to be indulged by their father and embarrassed to be "on show."

59

The twins caught each other's glance and started a game that only teenage boys would invent. The first boy started to convulse, shaking his arms, rolling his eyes back in his head, and he flopped onto the floor.

His mother screeched and put her hand to her mouth. "Jordan, what is happening to your boys?" she shrieked.

By this time, the second son was flopping against the wall, pretending to be losing control of himself.

"Okay, boys. Cut it out, now," their father said laughing. He got up and walked over to the boy on the floor. The kid stood up, laughing while his brother was bent over in hysterics. The brothers slapped each other on their arms, and the glint in their eyes indicated the high degree of pleasure they had taken in pretending to be drunk.

"Well, I guess this is a sort of celebration of things," Mr. Johnson said. "Texas is independent of Mexico, and my boys are growing up." He took the jug and handed it back to Chico.

"We need to be going on now," Tom said. "I think if you go down a ways to where the Navasota takes off at the Brazos, that water should be fine. I 'spect the Washington folks will be trickling back in here before long."

Mr. Johnson stood up and offered his hand to Tom.

"Thank you for your bread and water," he said. "My boys will not soon forget your kindness."

Tom shook Johnson's hand. He scuffed one of the boys on his head and commented what fine boys they both were. Charlotte and Elizabeth wished the family good fortune, and Chico held his jug tight to his torso as they all walked back to the Mexia wagon.

## Entering Robertson's Grant — May 13th

"Ahwoooo!! Whoo, whoo, whoooo!" A coyote howl came from the woods. It was so loud it could be heard over the rattle and roll of the wagon. It was broad daylight. Elizabeth thought it was too early in the day for coyotes to be active. Several times when the coyotes howled in the night the men went out to check the camp. Each time they came back and sat with their long rifles and seemed to take a longer watch of the woods. Elizabeth wondered if the cries were maybe signals coming from Indians she knew lived in these parts and not coyotes at all. But nothing was said, and nothing of Indians was seen . . . until several days up the Navasota.

On a morning when Tom rearranged the contents of the wagon, he made a point to reload several more pistols and put them in the back of the wagon. "You just keep a listen for trouble, ma'am." He said to Charlotte. "That woman can shoot," he told Elizabeth with a wink and a nod toward Mrs. Mexia. He helped the women back into the wagon. Tom remounted the horse, and Chico took his place on the bench in front. The wagon rolled slowly that day, along the Navasota River. The road was well worn, but Tom seemed weary.

"We won't be pushing so hard now," Charlotte said to Elizabeth. "It's hard on the wagon and on the mules. These four are young. We just bought them but no need to wear them down. A steady pace, and we'll be up into our colony soon enough. You doin' okay?"

Elizabeth replied, "Sure, I'm fine. I'm getting hungry for my family," she said, looking dreamily out into the fields as they passed.

After a quiet spell she continued, "Charlotte, I've been wondering. What brought you out here? How do you live without your husband? I mean, I know you have Tom and Chico, but how is it a woman so much on her own like you are . . . way out here? Why don't you stay in a town? Why are you way out here?"

Charlotte listened respectfully to Elizabeth's question. She nodded and put some thought into her reply. "It's much with me as it is with you, Elizabeth," she said. "That Santa Anna you talked about — my husband had dealings with him, going back many years. He is a very bad man. Wherever he goes, he makes life hard. My Anthony had many dealings with him." She paused and considered the merits of full disclosure of her family truth. "For a while he was good. At least he pretended to be. But after he gained control of the country he made life terrible for us in Mexico." She looked around at the provisions and the weapons next to her. "We hide our children many times, my son and my daughter." She took a pistol in her hands. "I learned to defend myself and my family. But when the threat seemed impossible, Anthony took us to New Orleans." Charlotte looked out the back, wondering how to explain the rest. "We stay as far away as we can, so he won't bother us."

"Uummm," Elizabeth said nodding as she listened. *New Orleans*, she thought. *This is a long way from New Orleans.*

Charlotte went on with her story. "We ran from him a few years ago. We still have that game, like a cat and a mouse. We have land near Mexico City, more land than here. But we're always on the run." Charlotte stopped talking and ran her fingers over the pistol lying next to her. "Our children are young ones. I don't want them living in fear, but sometimes I think they will want to leave Mexico City."

Elizabeth thought about the safety of her own infant grandson who she hoped was safe back in Gonzales by now.

"My husband is very good at making business," Charlotte said. "He is making a business with some men in Galveston. They bring beautiful things in from far-away places, and they buy land." The wagon rattled on as Charlotte remembered her husband's successes. "Anthony knows how to get along with people. He learns their languages so everyone can understand."

Charlotte pulled her knees up a bit and tensed her body. Her lips tightened. Her eyes took on the look of grit Elizabeth had seen in Elder John Parker's eyes during his most dramatic sermons. "Like you, we lost our oldest son." Charlotte paused to let that memory simmer. Then she continued, "The two children we have will inherit what we do out here, Elizabeth. This trip is for business, both for my husband and for my children. If I have to be on my own sometimes then that is a small sacrifice. Tom and Chico are enough for me."

Her eyes shot toward the driver's bench. She tilted her head and gave a quick nod in that direction. "Chico was going to be shot. His parents were our friends in Mexico. They protected us and gave us information that saved our lives. Then they were murdered for that. Chico was barely grown, and they took him. But friends broke him out of jail in Mexico City. Now we repay our debt to those friends and care for him. He is family to us. He stays in hiding when we go south. In secret he prepares for our next journey out here. He makes the pemmican and the pulque and his medicines. He polishes and sharpens his tools. He repairs things that are broken and even makes toys for my children. He is wonderful to us."

"Oh, my . . . I understand." Elizabeth spoke slowly. "Why does he have only one spur? It's so fancy. I thought they came in pairs and were used for herding cattle. He doesn't need a spur for the work he does, but it's very much a part of him, isn't it?"

"Chico comes from an old, influential Spanish family. Unfortunately for them their influence was considered betrayal. When Santa Anna took over, he eliminated anyone who crossed him. Chico has a brother. They share the spurs their father wore. It is a family tradition, and they wear them for their heritage, not for the work they would do. When we get near to Mexico City he takes it off. But out here he can let it sing out like his song of liberation."

Elizabeth was intrigued and felt a new admiration for the little man with the jangle in his step. She understood what she had seen Chico do by the fire, and she understood why he was so content with his role. They both sat quietly, their heads bobbing with the rhythm of the wagon.

After a long while Charlotte continued. "Chico loves coming out here. Out here he feels free. This land means life to Chico, and it will mean freedom to my children one day. We must all be generous with what we have, just as our friends have been generous with us."

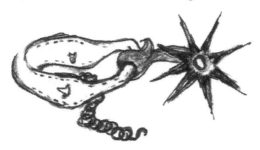

Elizabeth knew the impact of that generosity. She felt a sisterhood with Charlotte, humbled and grateful for the kindness that had brought her on this journey to find her family. "Yes," She said. "I'm blessed to have made your acquaintance."

"And I am blessed to have you as my friend, Elizabeth," Charlotte said in a quiet and sincere voice.

## Indian Encounter — May 14th

"Whoa!"

The mules slowed to a stop, and Chico reined in his horse.

Chico's voice was speaking words Elizabeth had never heard. It wasn't English, and it wasn't Spanish. It was a choppy, halting, guttural conversation.

"Indians," Charlotte said quietly. She raised her hand to tell Elizabeth to be still.

Men's voices continued to exchange the choppy phrases. Then Tom yelled out to Charlotte. "Mrs. Mexia, can you hear me?"

"Yes, Tom. I can hear you," she yelled back.

Elizabeth felt her heart pounding in her ears.

Slowly and emphasizing each word, Tom said, "Bring-me-that-leather-pass."

"Yes, Tom," she replied. In a motion that looked as if it was well rehearsed, Charlotte pulled up her knee and took off one of the heavy leather boots. From inside the boot she drew out a leather strap, looking to be just short of a foot long. She tossed it to her side as she pulled the boot back on her foot. Elizabeth could see in that brief time that the piece of leather was decorated with tiny blue-green beads. There were threads made of braided hair laced through the strap.

"What is it? What does it mean?" Elizabeth was intrigued, confused and curious all at once.

Charlotte grabbed it up and crawled to the front of the wagon. She reached out and handed the strap to Tom.

"You'll have to get out, ma'am. I'm sorry, but it's the only way," he told her.

"Yes, Tom." Charlotte crawled to the back of the wagon. In her haste she said to Elizabeth, "I'll explain later. We have to get out, but it's going to be alright. Just get out and don't say anything." Charlotte led the way, and Elizabeth followed her out the back opening of the wagon. The two women walked around and stood by Tom.

There in the road stood a tall, majestic Indian. Two more sat with their long, tawny legs wrapped around painted ponies. They all three carried long, slender lances pointed to the sky. Feathers tethered to the lances floated in the air above their heads. The man standing on the ground had thick, black circles painted around his eyes, and red slashes painted on his long, slender arms. Elizabeth took notice that his hands looked as big as his feet. His shoulders were broad and square. He squinted his eyes and frowned. Everything about him was ominous and threatening.

Elizabeth felt her gut tighten, and she found it hard to breathe. The tall Indian's long fingers were fondling the leather strap, while Chico looked toward him with an exaggerated smile. The Indian wasn't smiling. In fact, he looked most displeased.

He flung out his arms, shouting his choppy, halting words. Chico took him to the back of the wagon. The women could see that he pulled open the canvas and looked around inside. Elizabeth thought about her little travel bag. She expected him any moment to climb into the wagon and ravage the place, taking their treasures. But he just stood there, pensive as if he was calculating his options.

Chico and the Indian came around the other side of the wagon. Chico's eyes were wide, and his brow was wrinkled. "They want something . . . anything. They said they want a token of treaty between us."

"Do they recognize the leather pass?" Tom asked.

"Sí, but they think we stole it," Chico said.

Everyone was quiet, and Elizabeth remembered the coins she had tied in the seam of her underskirt. Without saying anything, she bent down to get it. The Indian jerked his head to look at her. She saw hatred in his eyes, and it was all she could do to untie the knot in the cotton under slip. The beat of her heart throbbed in her eyes, but she kept looking up at him. She worked her fingers as nimbly as she could. Then she felt the coins, and she presented one to him.

The Indian looked at the little coin in her hand. His face was stern, and his eyes glanced back at the wagon. Then he began to laugh. Elizabeth didn't know what to do, so she just froze with her hand outstretched, the coin sitting in her palm. Charlotte, Tom and Chico froze, too, not knowing what his laughter meant. The Indian said something to his companions, and they laughed, too. The Indian on the ground took the coin and inspected it. He looked back at Elizabeth and nodded slightly. He put the coin in his moccasin, and with very little effort remounted his horse. The three ponies pranced beside the wagon. The Indians barked a few more words at Chico, who glanced at Elizabeth, and then back at the men on the ponies. With that, the Indians went on their way. The travelers stood still until the Indians were out of sight.

"What was that about?" Tom asked Chico.

"They think the money was stolen, too," he said. "They think white man is a thief. They said the woman was just as bad."

"Get back in the wagon, and let's go," Tom said.

Once they were settled into place and the wagon began to roll forward, Elizabeth asked again about the leather strap. "What does it mean?" she wanted to know.

"That strap was given to us by some Comanches on our last trip out here. It is a sign of treaty to be shown for safe passage through Indian territory. Chico speaks their language, and he always has a way of pacifying them. A lot has happened since then with the war and all. You noticed the Indian kept it. We'll have to get another if we can. But Chico will take care of that. For now, we just have to pray."

With that Elizabeth's thoughts turned to her family and the church people who had come to this Indian territory years ago. She wondered what lay ahead, as their journey continued along the edge of the Navasota River.

## Finding the Parkers — May 16th

"Rest stop!"

It came time for Chico and Tom to switch drivers. Switching time always gave the foursome a chance to stretch their legs. Everyone crawled down and came around to the shade. Chico stretched backward with his arms held high overhead. "I'll check the team," he said to Tom.

Tom gave a nod and picked up a straight, pointed stick. He took notice that the earth here was much drier than the mud they left in their tracks farther south. This soil was saturated with the richness needed to support farmers in the area, if they lived long enough for a good crop.

He kneeled down on one knee and drew a straight line in the dirt, a line running south to north. Then he drew several short lines across it. "All goes right, today we get to the Parker place, ma'am," he said, directing his words to no one in particular. Then he scratched over all the lines he had drawn.

Tom stood up, threw down the stick and pushed the brim of his hat away from his face. He turned to Elizabeth and tucked his hands into the waist of his pants. "I been watching this territory grow for a few years. Your Benjamin described the clan that came out with your mother. I think I seen that camp before."

He turned and looked up the road. "They do church, and they're a bunch of brothers who farm on a big spread not far from the Mexia place. When we get there, we'll have to inquire. Some folks don't take to strangers asking about their business, but if it's your family we'll find out."

With that everyone got back into their places on the wagon, and they headed north again.

Elizabeth was too excited to speak. It was all she could do to contain her emotion. She felt every mile as the mules pulled them further north. And long before the sun went down, they approached a field of six working men. There was a big plow and a mule. A cart with tools sat near a towering post oak. Five men were in the field, too far out for conversation. Tom pulled the wagon up to a tree where one man was dipping water from a small barrel.

The man dipping water was bent and old. His hair was silver, and it hadn't been cut in quite a while. His face was craggy and burnt by the sun.

"Howdy," came the welcome from the old man. Elizabeth's heart skipped a beat. Could it be her family? She waited to hear more.

"Howdy to you all," Tom replied. "You live near here?"

"Well, we not just out here to pass the time o' day in this here field." The man laughed at his own sarcasm, and Elizabeth remembered Elder John Parker's sour wit. "What you folks need?"

"We're looking for the Parkers. Heard the whole family came out here. You know Parker?"

There was a pause. "Well, maybe. Who wants to know?" Elizabeth remembered the trouble that had plagued her Parker half-brother back in the states. That half-brother was also her brother-in-law now. He was married to Patsey, the sister she wanted most to see. James Parker was always evasive. Was it James at the cart?

"Well, we got somebody here belongs to the family," Tom said. "Sure be good if we can bring 'em together."

The man drinking water stopped moving. He didn't say a word for a long spell. He stood tall and looked straight ahead, as if he was taking mental inventory of the family members. Elizabeth's heart pounded. Charlotte held her breath. The two friends strained to look at each other from the corners of their eyes but stayed still so they could hear every word.

Finally, the man at the cart spoke. "I can tell the Parkers you bringin' someone in. Let me come over there and see so I can tell 'em."

"You come on, now. That be a good way," Tom said.

"I heard him, Tom. I'm getting out," Elizabeth shouted.

Then the old man spoke again. "You two men — you go stand aside." He waved Tom and Chico away from the wagon. "You tell your Parker party to come out alone."

Charlotte helped Elizabeth get out of the wagon. Elizabeth's knees were shaking. Her foot touched the ground, and she made a conscious effort to tighten her limbs. She clinched her teeth and closed her eyes. She said a little prayer that this was her family. With all the composure she could muster she calmed herself. She put one foot in front of the other. She held onto the wagon and came around to face the man who wanted to see her.

## Elder John Recognizes Elizabeth — May 16th

"Elder John?"

Elizabeth stood at the end of the wagon. It had been years since she had seen him. His hair was darker then, but his face was unmistakable. "Elder John?" she repeated.

He was walking toward the wagon. "Elizabeth? Is that truly you, Elizabeth?"

"Yes, sir, it's truly me," she said laughing, "and I'm truly glad to see you!"

"Well, I'll be a three-legged jackrabbit," he said. "Come over here and let me look at you, girl!"

She ducked her head feeling a bit shy, not really comfortable to be "on show." The old man turned to the field. By then the five men out there were curious to know what their leader was doing, and they were looking in the direction of the wagon.

"Come on here," he yelled, waving out to the field. "Look here who come to see us!"

The men came quickly and welcomed her.

"How did you find us?"

"Your mama's gonna love seeing you."

"What a surprise!"

Elizabeth was thrilled to see the men, but mostly she wanted to see her mother and her sisters. The old man finally gave in. "We're Parkers," he admitted to Tom and Chico. "I guess you know by now. It's about time we shut down for the day." He turned to Chico and Tom. "You go with us to the camp, and I'll ride with you. Come on men, let's call it a day."

Elder John Parker immediately extended Charlotte and her men an invitation to the Parker compound. The Parker men unhitched the mule from their plow and hitched him up to the cart with the supplies. They left the plow in the field, walked away, letting the mule lead them. Tom, Chico and Elder John followed in the Mexia wagon. Elizabeth rode in the back with Charlotte, unable to see the fortress until they were inside the gates.

When the wagon stopped, Elizabeth and Charlotte crawled out of the back and looked around at the massive walls surrounding the compound. Several acres were enclosed by jagged timbers. Heavy gates completed the security, and blockhouses guarded two corners. Little cabins lined the wall opposite the gates. Elizabeth remembered it all from her stay there a few years earlier.

One of the Parker men ran ahead of the cart, up to one of the little cabins. "Come out here," he yelled. "Patsey! Mama! Rachael! Come out here!"

Elizabeth stood next to her friend Charlotte and waited. She smoothed her skirt and held her hands together at her waist. She heard women's voices and saw two little children coming through the door of a cabin. Then someone she recognized, her sister Patsey, came into the big courtyard.

"Oh, Elizabeth!" Patsey ran to her sister and gave her a hug. "Mama, look who's here!" her sister yelled toward the cabin. Several little children came around and looked curiously at Elizabeth. Then Grannie Parker, a tiny, frail woman, emerged from the cabin.

Elizabeth had found her family. Years ago, back in Illinois, her widowed mother married Elder John Parker. At a time when North America was being redesigned by war and settlers, husbands and wives were taken early in the process. Life was hard and often short. Illness and accidents visited every family. Richard Duty and Sallie White Parker had gone to their afterlife as young parents. Elder John Parker and Sallie Duty married, which blended the two families. Then two Parker sons, James and Silas, married two Duty daughters, Patsey and Lucy. By these marriages the Parker-Duty clan expanded. Then the Parker men

71

established the Pilgrim Regular Predestinarian Baptist Church of Jesus Christ, and the population grew even larger. What Elizabeth found in the Parker Stockade that day was the Primitive Baptist community of folks from Illinois, transplanted to Texas in its entirety.

Sister Patsey was only a few years younger than Elizabeth, and they had been very close in childhood. But Patsey married trouble. James Parker was a strange blend of righteousness and rebellion. There had been questions about his integrity. When the girls' daddy, Richard Duty, was alive he had warned the girls to stay clear of James. But Patsey loved him, and love was hard to deny.

The Pilgrim Regular Predestinarian Baptists could provoke judgement in these lawless times. It was a fact that some members of this family had conducted themselves questionably at times. What family could deny making mistakes? Elizabeth figured the "questions" folks had about somebody else's business were irrelevant to her. Everyone had opinions. Elizabeth had developed a way of listening to those opinions without comment. She heard the condemnations, but she always wanted to hear the defense. And she always considered both sides.

After all the years of listening, she decided it wasn't her place to judge, and so she didn't. If Patsey loved James, there must be enough goodness in the man to warrant that love, and Elizabeth accepted him on that basis. She had decided long ago that James Parker was a good man who made a few mistakes like everyone else in the family.

As was often the case in those times, Elizabeth had a past that included a previous marriage. She was married a lifetime ago to William Griggs. During that marriage she had confided to Patsey that she wanted children. But as was seldom the case in those days of large families, Elizabeth remained childless. When Patsey had her first child, Rachael, they arranged their lives so Rachael could spend time with her Aunt Elizabeth. That was the only mothering Elizabeth had known as Mrs. Griggs, and she loved Rachael dearly.

Then Griggs died. Elizabeth lived as a widow until she married John Benjamin Kellogg. His son was just a few years older than Rachael. Elizabeth was thrilled to have a child she could call her own. For those brief years back in Illinois, the young cousins and their mothers had spent as much time together as they could. Those were precious and binding times. It was those memories that flooded her thoughts as Elizabeth embraced the women she loved. Sister Lucy was next in age, about four years younger than Patsey. Lucy Duty and her husband Silas Parker had four children by the day of this reunion. Cynthia Ann was the oldest at age nine, then John Richard, age seven, and two more toddlers. Elizabeth realized how much she missed and how much she wanted to know, as the young ones gathered in the main yard of the fort.

"Come in here and rest. You folks come stay the night," Grannie Sallie Parker said looking at Charlotte and her hired men.

"We always got room for more folks here," Elder John Parker added. "The boys will get together some beef, and we'll have a big cookout!"

Everyone began to scurry around to make a celebration of Elizabeth's return.

"Sister, come in here, and let's get you a fresh dress," Patsey said.

"I think I need one," Elizabeth laughed. "I wore this out of Gonzales," she said as she twirled a bit to let the skirt flare around her legs, and the coins in her underskirt flopped awkwardly. The skirt was ragged and muddy. The blouse was frayed around the neck, and a button was missing. The dishrag sleeves were frayed and ragged with holes at the elbows.

Elizabeth, Charlotte, Lucy and Patsey went into a little cottage built against the towering wall where the magic of a bath and clean clothes made Elizabeth feel new again.

When the women came back outside there were people running around everywhere. Elizabeth was having a hard time making out who was who. Some went into the cabins, and others went out a back gate. Men were cooking, children were playing and women were bringing all sorts of food to a long table sitting in the center of the yard. It was a delightful chaos. She just gave up trying to remember everyone and thought she would sort it out later.

# Part Three:
# Unexpected Journey

# The Reunion — May 17th

"I just want to sit and listen to you tell me about what you been doing in the last year," Elizabeth said to her sister Patsey. Elizabeth looked around her for a way to include Charlotte in the conversation. "Come share a bench with me," Elizabeth joked to Charlotte as they sat on a split log. Soon other logs and pallets were pulled into place until something of a community was formed-up, like the church meetings Elizabeth remembered in days gone by.

It was rare that Elizabeth enjoyed a crowd, but on May 17th her heart was made glad by the crowd of family, which was the best kind of crowd.

Grannie Sallie Duty Parker tried to manage the chorus of questions hurled around them. The tiny woman stood in the middle of the crowd and gestured with her hands as if patting down a newly finished quilt. "Everyone sit around, and we'll find out all about it," she said.

Patsey's oldest child Rachael — now a young married woman, last name Plummer — stood by her mother holding her toddling son, James Pratt. Elizabeth's niece — that pretty girl Rachael who had teased and ridden horses with John Benjamin Jr. a few years ago — shaded her eyes from the sun as she waited her turn to reunite with her aunt. The sun highlighted the golden strands in the young mother's red hair.

Grannie Sallie raised her hands again to bring a hush over the crowd. "Who is our guest?" she wanted to know as she leaned into the direction of Charlotte. "This is my friend, Charlotte," Elizabeth said. "I couldn't have found you without her. She has a place not far up the road." Elizabeth gestured to the north.

Grannie Parker leaned back a little, curled her fingers and put a hand on each of her narrow hips. "Takes a lot of doin' out here, don't it, Charlotte? We're gon'na try to make you comfortable for a rest before you go on. Your men and those mules need a bit of rest now. We hope you'll feel welcome."

Charlotte nodded her thanks and smiled at Grannie.

A young boy named John Richard was caught up in his curiosity.

He walked near to his aunt Elizabeth and bent straight forward. He squatted at the knees with his hands in front of him on the ground. He inched his hand close enough to touch Charlotte's leather skirt, and his fingers tested the nature of it. His older sister, Cynthia Ann, stood over him.

Cynthia put one hand on her brother's shoulder and shaded her eyes with the other. Their mother Lucy was the second of Elizabeth's sisters who married Parker men. It was a curious arrangement, three Duty women marrying three Parker men. But this curiosity had blended so many families it seemed a very good thing. The children knew their cousins as well as they knew their siblings. Everyone pulled together and helped. Nobody could ever feel alone in this family.

Lucy Parker pulled a pallet near her sister and motioned to her children to come sit with her. "Silas and I are so happy you can be with us, Elizabeth." Cynthia Ann and John Richard snuggled into their mother's arms.

Others began to close the circle of conversation, pulling themselves nearer to the two women on the bench. "How have you fared through the recent Mexican war?" Elizabeth wanted to know.

"We hardly knew there was one," Grannie said with a hearty laugh. Then she turned more serious. "Naw, really now, this far north, they didn't really bother us out here."

One of the women continued, "Indians, that's our main problem. But mostly we got that under control. When we got word of the Mexicans, we figured it was best to leave for a while. So we were on our way out, got to the Trinity camp. We heard of the victory down at the San Jacinto, so we came on back home."

"Now we're wondering about how this new government is going to work," another woman explained.

"We just got our papers straight for the land grants. Our men will need to learn about it, but right now the spring crops need puttin' in," someone said.

Lucy said, "With the rains this year, we lost a lot of seed. The men been tendin' those fields ever'day for weeks now. We're hoping for a really good crop of corn."

Elizabeth looked from one woman to another, remembering Gonzales and trying to grasp how it was they were safe here from Santa Anna's wrath. This Texas was a wide stretch of ground with enough space for folks to live in what seemed like different worlds. She was glad the fortress was spared the fires.

"How was it for you, child?" Grannie asked.

Elizabeth didn't know where to start. "It's all burned," she said. A gasp crept through the air as they turned to each other wondering exactly what she meant. They knew it couldn't be good.

Charlotte reached over and put her hand on Elizabeth's wrist. "Further south it's been very bad," she said, looking at her friend. She knew it wasn't her place to explain Elizabeth's nightmares.

"Benjamin is working to clean up Harrisburg. The city was totally destroyed," Elizabeth said, trying to think of how to back into the worst of it. "Gonzales... I have no idea..." She couldn't go on. They wouldn't understand, they couldn't if they weren't there to see what happened. Elizabeth looked at Charlotte and then at her sisters. Her face was contorted with pain, and tears flowed without control.

Young Rachael, wishing to improve the mood, mistakenly asked, "How is my cousin, Aunt Elizabeth? What is Johnny doing these days?" Elizabeth felt the innocent words stab into her heart. "Oh, Rachael," she gasped. That was her breaking point. She doubled over in pain and sobbed uncontrollably.

Rachael broke into tears and cried, "Oh, I'm so sorry, what did I say?" She tried to get up, but her skirt twisted around her knees. She stayed on the ground to avoid upsetting little James Pratt, as the children fell into a state of confusion over the show of despair. Half the women in the crowd were crying and consoling each other, still not knowing the facts. Charlotte stood up to explain what she knew.

"Your sister has been through hell." She said. Everyone went quiet and looked at her. She swallowed hard and took a deep breath. "The settlements down south were visited personally by the Mexican troops. Gonzales was one of the first . . . and one of the worst."

Charlotte bent down and put a hand on Rachael's shoulder. "Your cousin John Benjamin is gone, my dear."

Rachael began to shake her head in denial, her hand to her mouth, her eyes wide in disbelief.

"I'm sorry. It's true. He was at the mission in San Antonio, and they were all . . . ." Charlotte didn't want to say the word "killed." "They're all gone. No one came home."

Between her sobs Elizabeth began to share the horrors. "They told us to leave. We packed up and burned everything." Then she fell forward giving in to the desperation she remembered. Young John Richard turned away and reached up for his sister. Cynthia Ann took her brother's hand and walked him to the outer edge of the group. The children stood looking at their relatives' anguish, wondering what it all meant.

Charlotte knelt by Elizabeth, who had recovered enough to continue to speak. Sitting in the center of her family, Elizabeth finished her report. Wanting to address Rachael, for the sake of the precious history they shared, she looked at her niece and explained further. "Johnny had a wife. Her name was Sydnie. And she had a baby on the trail."

Everyone was quiet.

"Johnny is gone. Sydnie is gone. The baby went back to Gonzales with his grandparents." Elizabeth took a long, deep breath. "I'll go there, too. But for now, I just wanted to see you," she said. "I came here to find some peace, to be with the people I love and maybe rest a little."

Lucy stood up. "I think we understand now." She looked around. All was quiet except for the distant sounds of the men cooking. Elizabeth hoped Tom had explained her story to them. She didn't think she could repeat it again.

The sun was lower in the west, and the day was aging. There was a sense of completion in the family. This was a time for turning a page in time, to let the past go and look to the fields for new crops, new stories. No one wanted to drag the recent past along with them.

Grannie stood up, wanting to bring honorable closure to the episode. "We have much to be thankful for," she said. "This daughter has come for peace, and here we have peace. These walls are our shelter." She gestured to the towering, jagged posts. "Let's have good food and good words, and let the past be the past." She turned to Charlotte and Elizabeth. "We'll show you a space to stay the night, and tomorrow we'll start again."

The Parkers were good hosts. Tom, Chico and Charlotte rested and then went on their way. Elizabeth's soul began to heal. She began to believe that very soon she could go back to Gonzales with her husband and be a farm wife.

But that was not to be . . . .

## Finding Peace — Early Morning May 19th

On the nineteenth day of May, 1836, Clara Elizabeth Duty Kellogg was feeling safe for the first time in two years.

She sat in the massive courtyard with her sister Patsey and their mother. Life in general was turbulent in this territory, very near the terrible Comancheria. But James Parker, Patsey's husband, had made a personal treaty with the natives whose hunting grounds they shared. They made trade together.

In those days Indians obtained horses two ways — either they rounded them up from the wild herds, or they stole them. James bought their horses, and he never asked where they came from. James just wanted to keep the peace, to keep his family safe from Indian violence. If buying a few stolen horses kept the Indians happy with the Parkers, that was fine with James.

James paid for the horses with scrip from a bank in the United States. The scrip was old, but so far it was being honored at trading posts. The Indians valued it and had been happy with the arrangement. James bet his entire family and fortune on that happiness.

So it seemed clear to James that he wasn't a thief, and he wasn't a counterfeiter, though he had been accused of both back in the United States. James' conscience was clear. The Parker fortress had been established in Mexico, and out here the past didn't matter anyway. James was starting over.

Based on James' personal treaty with the Indians, the Parker women had come to feel safe inside the fortress built by their men. Within that security these women drew on a new sense of hope and happiness. The revolution was over, and Texas was free of Mexico. The air seemed fresher in the infant days of the newest nation on earth. The Republic of Texas was rising up from the waste of a brief war. Texans felt hopeful again.

Thirty-some humans, a blend of Parker men, Duty women, family and friends from both sides, inhabited the impressive stockade at the time of Elizabeth's visit. She was happy to just share a space with her family for a short time between Harrisburg and Gonzales. She wouldn't be here for long.

"Mama, I can't remember when I have felt so at ease," she said as the other women in the family casually went about the early morning routine. Elizabeth, her sister Patsey, their mother and the others sat just outside the open doorway of one of the cabins near the corner blockade.

"Rachael, come over here and let Elizabeth brush your hair this morning," Patsey said to her seventeen-year-old daughter. Rachael led James Pratt by one hand to her aunt. Rachael sat on the ground and lifted little James into her lap. She snuggled him tight and smiled with secret anticipation for the unborn baby in her little belly.

"Here's my hairbrush, Aunt Elizabeth. I like to brush it good before I tie it all up." Rachael had a shell comb in her hand she would use later to grip the heavy red curls into a bun.

Elizabeth took the long, thick auburn waves in her hands and pulled brush bristles through them, somewhat in awe of the beauty of her favorite niece.

After a thorough session of quiet brushing Rachael stood up and took her young son further into the courtyard to enjoy the fresh morning air. "We'll go check the garden," she called back.

Elizabeth and Patsey were alone with their mother. "Mama, I have something for you and for you, Sister. She picked up the tattered under skirt she had recently taken off, worked the hem of the cotton fabric and pulled out several coins. "Here, Patsey. Put these in a safe place." She handed her sister a handful of half-dimes. Then she searched the fabric for other coins. "Here Mama. These are for you," she said as she handed Grannie Parker a handful of the discs of precious metal.

"Where did you get this, Liz?" her mother asked wide-eyed as she and Patsey inspected the coins.

"When we left Gonzales, Mama. Johnny's wife worked in the general store. The town was buzzin' like a beehive with all the people there. Everybody was buyin' everything they needed, and there was such a run of goods, the till was full. When they burned the town, Sydnie and her friend 'Nita took the money. The men were gone. Everything was in such a state of chaos, they thought to at least make good use of what they could save."

"The men who owned the store went to San Antonio, and . . . well, they weren't ever coming back. Those two young gals had a long history with that store, and they believed the men would want the money to go to the town's people. They sure weren't going to just bury it and leave it behind. So they handed it out just before the fire."

Elizabeth ripped open the decaying fabric of her under skirt and gathered the last of the money.

"Everything was in such a state of confusion, I don't think the people even realized what the girls were handing out, but maybe they found it useful later. Anyhow, they brought me and Benjamin coins, and I want to share them with you. Benjamin is working now. I'm living with you for a while. This is a way to share, and that's what I want to do. Just put it in a safe place for now, and one day you may want it for something important."

"Thank you, 'Liz-beth. That's very generous of you," Patsey said as she put her coins into her skirt pocket.

Mama went to the big family trunk. "I'm puttin' my coins in here," she said. She opened the lid and dipped her head and shoulders into the thing. "Elizabeth, come hold this lid for me."

Elizabeth went over to help her mother. The older woman was so small, she bent at the waist and the top half of her body was lost in the space of the trunk. Elizabeth held the trunk lid open for her mother. She smiled at her sister, amused at their mother's comical situation. The old woman opened a small tin, dropped her coins into it and closed the tin lid.

Elizabeth rewrapped the other coins in the remains of her tattered underskirt and tossed the bundle to the bottom of the trunk. "I'll get them sorted out later, Mama," she said.

When the task was completed, they closed the lid and came back to sit at a table to finish their coffee. Patsey passed a pan of biscuits, and all seemed heavenly.

In a quiet place in Elizabeth's mind she imagined how life would be here without the protection of the stockade. She knew these prairies were Indian hunting grounds. She also knew about James' business arrangement with the Indians, and that seemed to give everyone a sense of confidence about their safety. She remembered Benjamin's prediction that if she could get to the fortress without Indians, she would finally be safe.

Elizabeth did feel safe that morning, even though she knew of a rumor of an Indian raid. Elizabeth was a good listener. The men didn't whisper like women, and Elizabeth overheard a conversation early in her visit.

Two men came to the family compound the same morning Charlotte and her men left. It was a white man with an Indian scout came to warn the family about an impending raid. Jonas, Silas and Benjamin had gone out to meet with them in the outer stockade while Elizabeth was sitting out there by the well.

After a quiet conversation became louder, James appeared agitated. "It's not for us to worry about," she heard James say. "They're not going to bother us." Silas looked around as if he had his doubts, but when he saw Elizabeth he dropped the conversation and walked away.

The Indian scout had news from the hunting grounds. He had heard a plot to raid the fort. The rumor spread quickly through the compound, and some of the members of the Baptist clan believed the warnings. They packed up and left that very day. But James would not believe the Comanches would strike the hand that paid them. He relaxed his vigilance.

What James didn't know was that when he had taken the last delivery of horses, he paid the Indians with scrip that was no longer being honored. The bank it was written on had folded, gone out of business. The paper was worthless. When the Indians tried to use it at the trading post, they were turned down. It wasn't intentional, but the Indians felt deceived.

Without that information, and with no sense of tension at all, the Parker women drank okra coffee, ate biscuits and brushed the children's hair.

The men went every morning out into their fields, and this day was no different. Today the morning was calm, and it passed quickly.

Elizabeth took a deep breath, sipped the brown beverage in her tin cup, and reveled in the pleasure of peace. She lifted her feet from the floor and propped them on a small stool. "What chores do we have this morning?" she asked her mother.

The words were barely out of her mouth when one of the men came screaming through the massive gates of the fortress. "Indians!" he warned. His face communicated terror. But the big gates to the fortress were still open, and no one seemed concerned to close them. Elizabeth stood to consider the situation.

## The Raid — Late Morning May 19th

"Indians!"

Silas Parker shouted his warning as he hustled back through the open gates of the stockade where several families prepared for their morning. The heavy double gates were intended to secure the fortress home of the Parker clan, but no one had bothered to close them on the night of May 18th, nor had any of the men closed them when they left for their field work, just within the last few hours. Several acres enclosed by a twelve-foot fence, two corner blockhouse towers and six tiny cabins along the walls—all this was designed for protection. But today it was left wide open.

"No, it can't be. Not now," Grannie muttered between gritted teeth. The panicked old woman raised her hands over her head and shook them as she ran to the massive family trunk and struggled to open the domed lid. Elder John Parker went to the back wall for his musket. Young mothers gathered their children, huddling together to await instructions.

Life in general was turbulent in the Comanche territory, but the clan inside the Parker fortress was of the belief that today of all days would be a peaceful one. It was a beautiful day in May. The whole territory had just overcome so much anarchy, they believed today would be a peaceful one. They were wrong.

Silas's brother Benjamin burst into the main courtyard of the fortress. Breathless, he held one hand to his chest and with the other he stretched an open hand out to calm the women. "I'm going out to see what they want." He said panting. "This ain't normal." He leaned against the stone wall of the well. "They have a white flag and they stopped to wait. If they wanted to raid us, they could have come in on us without stopping." He paused, bent over with his head down toward his waist to finally catch a good breath. "Now, just in case, you women take these young'uns and get to the woods."

The sound of anxious whispers and the scurrying of little feet swept across the space. The mothers herded their children to the back gate which would lead them unseen in the direction of the tree line behind the rustic prairie lodges. The bright eyes of the young ones were wide in panic. They knew their lives were at stake. The panicked mothers motioned them on. They all held a collective breath until they could disappear in the woods behind new spring leaves.

Elizabeth's niece Rachael Plummer had just returned from the garden with her son in tow. They glanced at each other, both knowing they needed to hasten their escape with old Sallie. "What are you doing, Grannie?" Rachael said.

The old woman had by this time climbed into the huge trunk and was throwing out what got in her way. "I had those coins, 'Lizabeth! I know I put it in here." Elizabeth looked at her niece hoping Rachael might know just the right way to coax the woman out of harm's way. Thinking she might buy them all some time, while Rachael tried to coax her grandmother along, Elizabeth ran to the open gates. She tried to close them, but they were too heavy. She paused to assess the situation outside the gates.

"What do you want?" she heard Benjamin say. He was looking up at two warriors. Elizabeth felt a heaviness in her stomach. The glare of the morning sun blinded her at first. She shaded her eyes with her hand, and then she was able to focus. There on his pony sat a man with huge hands. His arms were decorated with jagged red lines. And on his face were the thick black circles around his eyes. Had they followed the Mexia wagon here after the encounter on the trail?

The long lances were very much like those belonging to the Indians who took Elizabeth's coin. There were the feathers fluttering above their heads, tethered to the tips of the spears. And today a stark white banner waved among them. Could it be they came for a work of friendship? The women wouldn't take a chance yet on friendship. Elizabeth dashed back to make her escape out the back way with her mother and her niece.

"Mother, come on." Elizabeth tugged on her Mother's arms as Racheal helped lift the frail legs out and over the edge of the trunk.

The Elder John was cursing his missing gunpowder, arranging his wads and stuffing his pockets with balls of lead. "Damn them Injuns! They'll not run us out!" He seemed disconnected from concern for the women but focused on his weapon.

Grannie was still in her night clothes and seemed to not fully understand the urgency to leave. Rachael's toddler son, James Pratt clung to his mother's skirt. She picked him up and the three women finally began to make their way toward the back of the enclosure. But it was too late.

The women found themselves surrounded by a flood of ponies led by the same two warriors Elizabeth saw talking to Benjamin. Their upper bodies were painted and draped with ornaments. A breechcloth shielded them where they sat, and their lean, muscular legs told of their physical prowess. Now at a closer proximity she could see their faces. They were not there for friendship.

Elizabeth froze in place. She squared her shoulders and bristled. The leader wore a headdress of buffalo horns. He raised a lance and the ponies came to a halt. The second warrior wore a cascade of eagle feathers flowing down from the back of his head. He continued to walk his pony toward Rachael. Slowly she lowered her young son to the ground and he pulled his mother's skirt up under his chin. "Run to your grandpa, son." His mother whispered. With that, the child did as he was told, heading for the cabin on legs that barely knew how to walk. Dry dust followed him, and he disappeared into one of the six cabins built along the back wall of the fortification.

The warrior by then was only feet away from Rachael, and he seemed amused at her efforts to save the child. He raised his lance and spoke something which brought a look of smugness to his face. Several warriors left the enclosure. *RUN, little James. Run and hide,* Elizabeth thought.

While Elizabeth maintained her rigid stance, the warriors gave their attention to Rachael. This American beauty would have attracted men of any background, and she must have appeared a rare sampling to men who collected scalps. Rachael's hair was red ochre, and it fell in waves from her crown past her shoulders. Any other day she might have tied it up, but this morning's unexpected raid caught her with it down.

The warriors nudged her with their feet, causing her to stumble along from one pony to another. They leaned over and tugged her by her hair, laughing and conversing together as if plotting something wicked. She lost her balance and they dragged her. One of the Indian women ran between the ponies and thrashed Rachael on her back with the blade of a garden hoe. Elizabeth feared for her niece's life, but she knew she had nothing to offer in exchange. She closed her eyes and turned away, clinched her teeth, kept her silence and stood firm.

Suddenly an overbearing warrior turned his attention to Grannie. He leaped from his pony and landed in front of her. She grasped at her gown and seemed to shrink as he gestured with his arms. In an instant three more natives dismounted and ran at her, pushing her to the ground. By then a crazed Elder John was swinging the butt end of his weapon in his wife's defense.

Elizabeth turned her head away and refused to know what all the vicious noises meant. There were cries of pain and shrieks of violence, the neigh of ponies and the clamor of hooves against the dry ground. It seemed to go on for a painful eternity. Grannie screeched; Elder John groaned and cursed. Elizabeth thought anyone for miles around surely would hear the pleas for mercy and come to offer help, but no one came. Then their steady whoops sounded like a victory chorus, and Elizabeth opened her eyes.

Grannie was pinned to the earth with lances. They pierced her garments, and blood pooled from under her on the ground. Elizabeth couldn't know how much flesh was cut beneath the fabric. Her mother was moaning, and Elizabeth wanted to reach down and help her. More than anything she had ever wanted in all her years, Elizabeth felt the need to be bold, to defy these men and go to her bleeding mother. But a wisdom guarded her against the emotion. She maintained her statue-state. Elizabeth had spent a lifetime minding her own business.

Today, though it sickened her, she kept that tradition, and it would be the one thing that saved her life.

The Elder John was near his wife, but mutilated. He was stripped bare. From Elizabeth's vantage point he looked like a butchered animal with his legs a-tangle.

Several painted warriors came to Elizabeth then. The Indians' arms were painted with jagged lines in red and black. Her eyes fixed on those lines as the men wrapped twine around her wrists. She saw tucked into the waist of a loin cloth a mass of silver hair attached to bloody flesh. It was the Elder's scalp. She never gave them reason of concern for her movement, as she had been frozen in place for all this time.

Rachael, however, was crying, wailing, gesturing and cursing them for their cruelty. Rachael's defiance was clearly a trigger for retribution. The woman with the hoe smacked Rachael in the face. Her head pitched back, and blood gushed from her nose and mouth. The mass of thick red hair wrapped around Rachel's face as she fell to the ground.

A brotherhood of braves grabbed at Rachael, forcing her to stand. They bound her wrists, and a cord of leather was tied around her head. The long strap was wedged between her teeth, holding her mouth open, preventing her from using her tongue or making any purposeful conversation. After the binding was complete the warriors remounted their ponies and led the two women with their ropes. Grannie was left moaning on the ground. The awkward procession left through the open gates out into the prairie beyond what was believed to be a secure home.

What Elizabeth saw next was beyond belief. Horsemen by the hundreds — maybe a thousand — she didn't think she could count them all. The savages had found three children. A girl and two little boys were screaming from the clutch of their captors. Elizabeth's brother-in-law Benjamin was laying on the ground, pierced through with so many spears. His head was distorted and bloody.

The proud victors stood over him, arrogantly making a show of their prowess as they reclaimed their weapons. Their companions celebrated each time a spear was pulled out from his flesh, dripping with Benjamin's blood and tissue. Several savages waved scalps in their celebratory carousing.

Trying not to make a display of her revulsion Elizabeth kept her head down, discretely glancing around the field from the corner of her eyes. Other bodies were slumped in awkward contortions where they lost their last efforts to live. She couldn't remember who had gone to the fields and who had stayed inside the compound this morning. She only knew that death had ridden in on horseback and life as she knew it had turned dark again.

# Part Four:
# A Captive's Journey

## A Terrible Vision — Evening May 19th

"Mira . . ." Chico nudged Tom's knee and pointed out toward the flat plains that made up the land they camped upon. "Qué es eso?" Without looking at Tom, Chico strained his eyes to see the peculiar procession making its way along the flat edge of the horizon. Then he turned to Tom with his question displayed on his face. "What is that? What can it be?"

Tom put down the weapon he was cleaning. He stood with his mouth agape and stared in the direction Chico had indicated. After several seconds he took a ragged breath and pointed out there, as if seeing an apparition. "Oh, my god," he said quietly. "What the . . . ." He hustled to his knapsacks and located the monocular Anthony Mexia had recently brought from New Orleans. With the sun behind him he walked east and lengthened the tube he hoped would enlarge the curious scene in the distance. He had an idea about it, but he hoped he was wrong.

"Go get Miss Charlotte," he told Chico, as he continued walking, one eye closed and the other peering into the looking glass. He had to be sure. He couldn't stop short and make a mistake.

Chico and Charlotte were standing by the wagon when Tom decided he had seen enough to confirm his fears.

"I do believe it's a raiding party, ma'am." He said as he approached them. They all began thinking about what that meant for their camp. When he reached them, Tom turned and looked again through the glass out to the eastern horizon.

"They're not comin' our way. I think they already did what they came to do. Looks like they have captives."

He handed the looking glass to Charlotte who looked through it in a panic.

Tom and Chico looked at each other. This was not a common experience. There was no established procedure for this like there was for escaping highway robbers on the trail.

They all stood and looked out at the line moving along the prairie and the shallow trail of dust rising from it as it moved northward.

The land Tom, Chico and Charlotte came to visit was rolling black land prairie, fringed with Indian grasses that blew sweetly in a summer breeze. They made their camp in one of the scattered stands of post oak. A person could maintain secrecy under the cover of the trees and still see for miles in the high elevation of those flat prairies. With his monocular Tom had a clear, uninterrupted view of the Indians in the parade out there on the horizon.

The Indians Tom saw were not the farmers whose villages were close by. No, those trotting in the parade were dressed for war. There were hundreds of them, just passing through. Tom thought he saw two women in the line, being led on ropes. The hair of one woman might have been red, or maybe it was just bloody. Either way, it wasn't a good thing.

"Miss Charlotte," Tom started, "I'm thinkin' about where these Indians could be comin' from."

The three of them quietly looked out to the prairies and tried to put the clues together.

"There aren't a lot of homesteads out that way," he pointed to the south.

Charlotte nodded her head slightly, realizing the only neighbors she knew were the Parkers. They lived to the south, and that was the direction the Indians were leaving.

"Do you think we might check on the them down in the fortress?" she asked Tom. "That's not even a day's ride," she reminded him.

Tom looked out at the horizon again. The parade of bodies jogging along was coming to its end. He was trying to imagine what might await him if he did go.

Finally he said, "I think they already did what they wanted to do. I'll go when the sun goes down."

## The First Thirty Miles — May 20th

Elizabeth staggered barefoot along the trail, being pushed and shoved as she stumbled along trying to keep up and stay calm. She hadn't put Sydnie's shoes on yesterday morning, and today she would regret that.

The Indians paraded single file along a path they knew well. It seemed to go on forever.

The raid at the Parker's fortress was conducted by hundreds of Indians. Apparently, the Comanche took issue with James' business practices. Much as the settlers would do, the Comanche recruited their friends and neighbors for assistance to claim justice. Gradually through the first night, the Keechi—having fulfilled their part—dropped out of the parade and just disappeared into the woods. The Comanche were the directors of this campaign, and they were the most numerous. The smaller contingent of Kiowa would stay with the Comanche until the job was completed.

When the full moon was directly overhead, they reached a camp that had been prepared by Kiowa women waiting for their return. The Indians gathered into three separate groups, two Comanche bands and one Kiowa. Elizabeth and Rachael collapsed to the ground.

The captive children were crying pitifully. Rachael called back to her young son. The woman with the hoe dragged the little boy by his arm and squatted with him just out of range of his mother, taunting them both. The child's arms stretched out in desperation to her, but Rachael couldn't reach him.

Several long, lean Comanche warriors came nearer, and Elizabeth hoped they might let Rachael loose to take little James Pratt. But no. They bound Rachael even more severely. They bent her over to lash her wrists to her ankles. They shoved her over, and she fell onto her face.

Some of the Comanche women gathered around Rachael. They started a dance, which evolved into a stomping. They started jumping on her legs, and she rolled to avoid them, so they stomped her body. The woman who had used the hoe dragged a fallen limb and beat her again. Then several of the women lifted her by her arms and took her away to their part of the camp.

*They'll kill her,* Elizabeth thought.

Meanwhile some chunky male Kiowa warriors dragged Elizabeth by her ropes to a part of the camp occupied by Kiowa women. Elizabeth managed to scramble onto her knees. Her skirt was torn, which allowed her to crawl. The rough ground bit into her knees.

She concentrated on the pain because she didn't want to hear the children crying or think about what was happening to Rachael. Finally, they stopped pulling her. She rolled into a ball and put her hands over her face.

Elizabeth's keepers had been waiting for the return of the men from the raid. The women jerked her up and pushed her toward a tree. They laced a leather rope between her tied hands and threw the end of it over a tree branch.

They pulled her up. She stood, but they kept pulling. She stretched, but they kept pulling. Her shoulders came up to her ears, and they kept pulling. They pulled until her feet were barely touching the ground.

Elizabeth didn't have food or drink all day, and she wondered about the others from her family. The children needed water. She knew they were all exhausted, hungry, thirsty and aching from their abuse.

Then the separate groups of Indians all came back together. Elizabeth smelled meat cooking. The women who strung her to the tree left their camp to share the celebration. Elizabeth was left alone. They stomped the ground and sang their haunting songs. They bellowed out their celebration. The children screamed for their mother, and the Indian women screamed back at them.

*That's a devil's chorus*, she thought.

The sky had been dark for a long, long time. Strung up from a single tether, Elizabeth's bare feet touched the ground below her with no space to spare. Her arms and shoulders ached, and her hands were going numb. Gradually the feasting and dancing quieted to a mild chant. The Indians went to their soft pallets of buffalo skin and went to sleep, as Elizabeth stood all night, her arms tied up in the tree.

## Charlotte's Reality — Midday May 20th

It was mid-day when Tom returned to the camp on the Mexia place. "It's terrible," he said as he got down from the mare.

Charlotte took the reins and stroked the animal's neck as she listened to Tom tell what he had seen.

"Everybody's gone," Tom said. Chico came and took the saddle off Tom's horse. He stood waiting to hear, too.

"It's a graveyard over there. Bodies everywhere. It was too dark for me to do anything, and I knew I needed to get back to you." He sat down. Chico took the saddle away.

Charlotte's eyes flitted from left to right, trying to imagine what her friend had experienced and what she might do to help in any way. Images came tumbling into her head. Tom hoped she hadn't seen the women on the ropes in the procession, but he didn't dare ask her.

"Did you see Elizabeth? Was she there?" Charlotte asked, not daring to ask directly if her friend was among the bodies.

"I don't know. I don't think so. I'll go back sundown tomorrow," Tom said. "I'll travel in the night and stay through the next day. I'll see what I can do then. From what I saw, there isn't much to be done. They're all gone."

It was one of those times in Texas when people with good intentions found themselves with few options. The Mexia team had come to Texas to meet the man who would confirm the boundaries of their land. And in reality, it wasn't "their" land.

The land being surveyed had been claimed by friends of Anthony Mexia and put into a trust for the Mexia children. Charlotte was certainly dedicated to her husband's business, but she was even more dedicated to the future welfare of her children. And she was painfully aware of the importance of loyalty among friends. Friends had been the redemption of the Mexias many times. But Mexias had also known the pain of betrayal. And now Charlotte was concerned that her friend Elizabeth might need her, and she wanted to be loyal. She struggled to know what she could do.

"We have to meet the surveyor here," Tom said. "I'll go see what I can do to help at the Parker place, but we can't abandon this land project."

Charlotte nodded her head. It wasn't the first time her options had been difficult, and she knew it probably wouldn't be the last.

## The Square People — May 21st–23rd

KERTHUMBLE!

Elizabeth Kellogg fell in a clump to the ground. The women were loosening her tethers. She opened her eyes to see the fleshy women standing over her. She saw her arms, but she couldn't feel them.

Unable to move she sat waiting, wondering what they would do to her now, and what they had done to Rachael and the children. Elizabeth was so numb she couldn't feel the women pushing her. They dragged her closer to the tree. They used the space where she fell to make a pile and organize their things. She was glad to be left alone.

She watched them. The women who tied Elizabeth were not like the Indians who took Rachael. No, there was a distinct difference.

The Comanche people were a handsome lot, and the men flaunted it. The warriors who took Rachael were naked except for their breech-

100

clout. The men had long hair to their waist or longer. Their heads were ornamented with feathers and metal ornaments woven into their long locks. They were painted with wide jagged lines and circles on their arms and bodies. In Elizabeth's conservative mind they were outrageously ostentatious.

Their women dressed and behaved as if they had been consigned to second place. Their hair was chopped off short, sticking out in all directions. Compared to the men, Comanche women were less flamboyant, with their simple dresses. Their long skirts made no restriction on their aggression. Those women in dresses had participated in the raid as forcefully as the men, behaving as if to win respect by their ability to inflict pain.

The Kiowa women who hung Elizabeth in the tree had been waiting in their camp during the raid. They were of shorter, stockier build. *Those women are almost square,* she thought. Their hair was thin, parted in the middle. The hair framed their faces and hung just short of their neck. Some of them were naked, decorated with thin lines tattooed into their skin. Their breasts and torsos were tattooed with thin lines making circles and triangles. Others wore dresses, but their faces, too, had thin lines running down their noses and lines from their eyes to the side of their head. Elizabeth imagined how long it must take and what pain to endure to accomplish all that tattooing.

She felt a tingle begin in her arms and in her back. The rush of blood was a welcome sensation, and she flexed her fingers. She shrugged her shoulders and tried to lift her hands over her head, but they couldn't go that far. The pain in her back was too intense. She'd try again later.

As Elizabeth sat on the ground, the square women rolled their buffalo hides and tied them just so. They organized their few belongings and put everything in a pile in their separate section of the camp near the tree where Elizabeth was waiting.

They chattered like chipmunks, talking their private talk. They hovered around Elizabeth, removed the long leash that had held her up in the tree and tossed it in their pile. Her hands had regained feeling. Now they were swollen and painful. They were still tied, and they would stay that way for the second day.

One of the women brought a small gourd of water. The women discussed something together, and the gourd was lifted to Elizabeth's lips. She pushed it from the bottom and slurped to get as much as she could into her mouth. She began to cough, and they took it away. She licked her lips and felt grit between her teeth.

There was no organized morning meal or ritual, no breakfast and certainly no coffee, nothing except the preparations to go. And so they went, out onto the prairie for the second day of walking even farther away from the fort.

This was the pattern for as long as the Comanche led the raiding parties home. Each night Elizabeth was strung-up, barely able to touch the ground. She was under the control of the same square, decorated women, and Rachael stayed under the authority of the lean women. The mixed band kept a steady pace going northeast each day. They would occasionally step out of line to pluck something from the woods to eat, or for "nature's call." But the line kept going.

Elizabeth passed the days without much food or water. On the trail they ate berries, leaves and sometimes snails, so Elizabeth did the same. But at night when the captors had a feast, their captives did not share. Elizabeth surprised herself to realize she was surviving. She imagined what it would be like to live this way. She wouldn't like it, and she prayed it was temporary.

Finally, one night things changed. All the different Indians circled around a fire, and there was more dancing. Elizabeth and Rachael were plopped near enough to hear each other's voice. "Oh, Elizabeth, what have we done?" Rachael said. "Hold on," Elizabeth replied. And that was as much as they could exchange before the stomping began again.

The three children were brought to the camp, all tied together. They all cried. The oldest was a girl, Cynthia Ann. She was holding her young cousin, James Pratt, with a rope tied from his foot to her wrist. When Rachael saw them, she wailed and tried to get up. The women knocked her down and jumped on top of her. At that point another group of women knocked little James from Cynthia's arms. He fell to the ground, and his cousin fell near him. The women gave all the children a thorough thrashing.

Elizabeth realized there was nothing she could do to help the children. She turned her head and tried not to know. She felt ashamed and helpless. She was sure they would all die before the night ended.

The men danced. They all ate and drank and threw scraps at their captives. It was the most food Elizabeth had access to since her capture. As the night went on the Indians went into a state of drunkenness, maybe from their exhaustion, or from their sense of victory, or from some intoxicating potion. Whatever the reasons, the celebration went on all night.

Elizabeth remembered the dogs she had kept back home. Now she was the dog and knew that life itself depended on what food she and the other captives could scrape off the ground. They cowered and scrounged. She was glad for the drunkenness, and everyone in the crowd seemed more interested in the orgy than in their captives.

Finally, the sky turned pink. Just as Elizabeth began to wonder what the day would bring, the square women came to get her. But this morning was different. The band of people broke into three separate groups and sorted their things.

Then the two warriors who had started it all—one still wearing his eagle feathers and the other carrying his buffalo horns—those two mounted their ponies in the center of the camp. Other men brought all the captives near the center. Their leader put the buffalo horns onto his head, and he raised his giant spear. He spoke in a language Elizabeth found vulgar and jagged, pointing the spear here and there.

Rachael was taken to one of the three camps, to the long, lean Comanches. A woman in that camp held little James Pratt.

Nine-year-old Cynthia Ann and her little brother John Richard were taken to a second camp of Comanches and given to other long slender people.

Elizabeth was taken by the square women who had strung her up every night in the third camp.

It was decided. The captives were divided up and parceled out to the various participants. The business was over. They simply turned their backs and left in three directions, finished with each other.

## Leaving the Comanches — May 24th–26th

"Can't you see, I need food?"

Elizabeth put her tied hands to her mouth, trying to mimic the sign language of her captors, but they paid her no mind, either because they didn't understand or because they didn't care. She suspected the latter. But she couldn't just stay mute any longer. She shouted at them in English, knowing they didn't understand her.

They continued to walk. When they stopped each night, they tossed her scraps after their evening meal and brought the water gourd. The tribal people understood each other but didn't care to communicate with Elizabeth. If they wanted her to walk, they shoved her. If they wanted her to stop, they shoved her. If they wanted to tie her to the tree, they shoved her. Shoving seemed to be their way of communicating with her, and she knew better than to shove them back.

On the first night away from the other bands, the square women didn't hang Elizabeth in a tree. She was tied to a tree trunk and allowed to sit on the ground.

The treatment she had before left her feeling damaged in her bones. As she went through her days now, her arms didn't work. She could reach her face with her hands in front of her, but she couldn't lift her arms over her head. Now that the square people were away from the others, they behaved differently, and Elizabeth was thankful. She was able to sleep for three nights with her arms tucked close to her body.

## Keeping Track of Time — May 24th – 29th

The Kiowa stirred with the first light. They were moving as soon as they could see a hand in front of their face. Day after day they packed and moved into the rising sun. They were well on their way before the heat embraced the earth. Their steps took on a rhythm, and they kept that walking beat until the sun set low at their backs.

Elizabeth began to wonder how long it had been since she was taken captive. She needed to keep track of the days. On the first day's journey away from the others—when she first started her journey with only the square people—she put a small stone in the hem of her torn under skirt. She tied that part into a tiny pocket in the seam, just as she had hidden the coins back in Harrisburg.

Each morning when the square women were packing Elizabeth chose a timepiece from the ground; a stone, a shell, a sturdy bit of a broken stick. She didn't know where she was going, but at least she would know when she got there how long it had taken.

The prairie at the fortress had been grassy plains with clusters of hardwoods. But going east the open plains gave way to thicker woods. The woods gradually closed in with broader stands of tall, slender pines. They were shaded most of the day, except for brief segments of trail where the sun peaked through the trees.

On the morning Elizabeth put the third timepiece in her hem-pocket, she was tied to a tree with long needles. As she worked the fabric, she caught a whiff of the pine. She secured the timepiece, tied the knot and sat up straight. She closed her eyes and took in the spicy aroma of the forest. When she opened her eyes she realized one of the Indian women was watching her. The woman came nearer and gestured toward the trees. She smiled, as if to say, "yes, doesn't it smell wonderful?"

Elizabeth wanted to believe she was seeing an act of friendship, but when she moved her pain and her restraints reminded her she was still a captive. *They aren't friends, no matter the smiles*, Elizabeth thought. *Why does it have to be this way?* She wondered. *What have I done to them? What do they want from me?*

The smiling woman came to the tree and loosened Elizabeth's ropes. *That was nice*, she thought. *They do have some compassion.*

The Indian chanted something. She leaned in close and spoke softly, as if she was confiding to her captive. Elizabeth was allowed to walk that day without being tied, but the smiling woman always stayed closed enough to grab her if she tried to run away. Elizabeth thought about it often, but every time she chose not to run.

Elizabeth felt confused. It was profound to her that the square women treated her differently now that they were away from the others.

On the day Elizabeth put the fifth timekeeper stone in her hem the caravan arrived at a camp on the Neches River, a beautiful ribbon of moving wetness. She could smell it before she saw it. The camp was occupied by old people and children who welcomed their warriors and women back home. Those less capable of aggression stayed behind while their young, strong ones went with their Comanche allies to raid the Parkers.

These were the Kiowa band who had migrated south many generations ago. With ancient roots as far north as Canada, they had tried to assimilate into the Black Hills of South Dakota where they discovered the advantages of riding horses. South Dakota was full of Indians back then. Several Indian nations competed to control the same hunting grounds there.

The Kiowa were a small community, outnumbered by all the others. Being at the mercy of the others, the Kiowa learned the merits of diplomacy and commerce. They learned to negotiate and trade. But that didn't secure their place in the Indian society. The other, more overbearing tribes assaulted them from all sides. Finally, the Kiowa gave in and migrated to Mexico.

They first fell in with the Wichita near the Red River. But as time went on, they moved further south along the Neches. And that's where they were when they brought Elizabeth to their camp.

The Kiowa learned from their history. They had to get along with their neighbors. Across the expanse of northern Mexico, everybody was a neighbor. And so, when the Comanches invited a tribe to partner with them on a raid, the Kiowa knew it was the neighborly thing to do.

These people were survivalists. When they weren't raiding with the neighbors, their men hunted, and their women gathered. Their old people minded the children, who played games with sticks and big pieces of cloth. The families were tight. Cousins, aunts, uncles and grandparents all lived together and took care of each other. Even the family dogs were prized members of the clan because they helped to carry supplies at moving time.

Their tipis were large structures made of long poles covered with soft leather. They were large enough for the extended families to all live together. The Kiowa were seasonal movers, as compared to their Comanche allies. Those Comanche moved like the wind, as constant as the floating leaves in the fall. But the Kiowa camped for a full season before moving on, so their homes were more substantial.

As the raiders returned to their camp, several women were sitting on large stones working with hides. They all stopped their work and gawked. The parade coming in walked directly to an old man sitting alone outside his tipi. He slid a short, braided rope in his fingers and muttered to himself. The square woman who had smiled at Elizabeth jabbered and bowed and pointed to him and pushed Elizabeth toward him as he stood up.

He poked at her, lifted her hair and examined her much like she thought he would examine a horse. In the end he seemed unimpressed. He shook his head with the universal "no." But the square women were unconcerned. They walked Elizabeth through the camp like a prized mare.

Back in South Dakota the Kiowa learned the merits of bartering. When they moved to Mexico, they found their neighbors appreciated a good deal in trade. Bringing in commodities from raids paid off in this territory, and Elizabeth had become a commodity.

The raid at Parker's fortress on May 19th was conducted by several bands who, like the white men of that time, were loyal to each other in their desperate clutch to hold onto their lands. The Indians found safety in numbers, just as all humans do. In that way, the Kiowa, the Comanche, the Keechi, the Wichita were not unlike the white pioneers trying to pursue life as they knew it. Elizabeth was getting a glimpse into the strategies of her captors, with their partnering in raids and trading their loot.

There were four-hundred-thousand square miles of land to be had in the northern regions of Mexico. The Indians had always "owned" it all. The Spanish tried to avoid them, and the Mexicans had left them alone for hundreds of years. When the white men came from the United States more recently, the Indians tried to share, but in their view the immigrants took more than their fair portion. These new neighbors were more difficult. Elizabeth figured the Indians were probably as confused as she was about their relationship with the meddlesome settlers.

The first night at the Neches, Elizabeth was allowed to sleep loose on the ground. They tied her feet and looped them loosely to her tied hands. But they didn't hang her, and she wasn't tied to a tree.

Things were improving for her, if just a little. Rather than throwing her scraps, they handed her a chunk of meat for her supper. It was more food than she had eaten since she left the fort, and it filled her stomach quickly. There was no dancing or stomping.

The women spent their days scraping the animal skins and gathering berries, seeds, and nuts to feed the children. The men made short hunting treks into the nearby woods, bringing home small game for the night's supper.

When the sun went down, the clan members made little campfires, roasted meat and chatted. The woman who smiled at Elizabeth pulled a buffalo hide next to the flap of her tipi and signaled for Elizabeth to stay there.

## The Second Judgement — May 30th

Elizabeth was confined to her buffalo blanket, and she was left alone for several days. In her alone time, she began to ruminate. *What are these people thinking?* she wondered. She noticed some likenesses between the Indians and herself, but the differences were greater. *Will it ever be possible for the farming immigrants to live alongside the "naturalists?" Can we ever live together in peace?*

The clan was usually still asleep when Elizabeth awakened in the mornings. Gradually they awakened and pattered casually around the camp. No one was going anywhere. She tried to pull her hair behind her head, out of her face. The damage to her back was so severe her shoulder joints just wouldn't work anymore. She could only reach her hair if she bent her head down to meet her hands.

A low ring of stones was constructed in the center of the camp where men often sat. There were large blackened chunks of wood in the middle of the ring. The community had a fire there each evening

On the days Elizabeth was left alone, occasionally someone would come and look at her. They would talk to each other and point to her, but no one tried to communicate with her. They brought her food and let her sleep, all in the same place.

At times, the woman who smiled would look at Elizabeth's arms and poke around on her flesh. They held sticks up to her feet and her hands, as if measuring her. It seemed they were fattening her, just letting her eat and sleep. Elizabeth didn't want to imagine what they had planned for her. The smiling woman began to raise Elizabeth's arms as if to test her ability to lift them herself. But they would flop back down.

One morning the women got up earlier, and they awakened her with tugs at her feet. They were untying her ankles. Then they untied her hands.

They took her to the river and began to pull at her clothes. She tried to resist, but there were too many. They ripped off the dress her sisters had given her at the fort. For a woman who valued her privacy, the exposure was humiliating. She was grateful that she was only exposed to the women; no men came to the river with them. She was shoved into the water, and the women splashed her and pushed her head under the water. Fortunately, the river wasn't deep there at the edge, and when she stood up, she could breathe.

The other women also stripped down for a bath. In spite of the shame she felt, Elizabeth looked at the black markings on the women's bodies. Then it occurred to her, what if they intended to mark her in the same way? While the water sloshed, and the women yakked, Elizabeth began to imagine what might be in store for her. *Are they going to tattoo me?*

She looked beyond the banks of the river. Could she run? No, it was impossible. The river was too wide, and water was deeper beyond the trough where she stood. *I'll just have to endure their torture,* she thought. *It won't be worse than hanging from a tree all night.*

The woman who smiled at her in the previous days rebound her hands, but loosely. Then she laced a leash to Elizabeth's wrists in order to lead her out of the water. Other women pushed her from behind, and together the wet mob slogged out of the river. They shook their heads to fling the water from their chopped hair and made their way back to the camp. Elizabeth's long hair was a wet tangled mass. It hadn't been brushed since she left the fort.

Elizabeth tried to hide her nakedness between the four women who stayed with her while the others ran ahead. She brought her elbows together as close as she could and held her hands over her face, trying to minimize her exposure.

Back at the camp, Elizabeth squatted on the buffalo hide where she had spent her free days. It smelled of urine and onions, but it was her special safe place. She kept her hands over her chest and cowered back into place. The square women went into their tipis and redressed. The sun felt good that day, as she was left naked to dry.

Then three women came to her, pulled Elizabeth up and wrapped her in a skirt like their own; a simple wrap of soft leather with a small flare on either side. The skirt wrapped around her waist, tied at the side, and fell just below her knees. *That's half a comfort,* she thought. *If they would only cover my chest.* She kept her arms over herself, holding her hands at her neck.

Then they gave her a pair of leather moccasins. Just a simple wrap of leather as soft as bunny ears. The feel of the smooth leather on her feet made her swoon. In spite of the abuse she had taken, if anything would make Elizabeth believe these people had heart, it was those moccasins. She closed her eyes and wiggled her toes. But the pleasure was short-lived.

Several of the women came around Elizabeth and began to pick at her hair with a thin stick. It pulled and hurt her scalp. For some reason they were pulling the tangles out. Then she realized they were braiding her hair. She had never worn her hair in braids, but it was long enough, once the mats were loosened.

As the braiding went on a chaos arose. All the children and some of the Kiowa braves were going toward the river, all yelling and waving their arms. Riders were coming toward the camp. Three riders came leading two more ponies and they carried several bundles.

The women seemed excited. They ran around the camp, leaving only one woman to plait Elizabeth's hair. Elizabeth took notice that she was weaving some feathers into the braids.

Elizabeth was becoming more and more uncomfortable with her nakedness, and then she had an idea.

As the women ran around welcoming the visitors, and the one woman plaited her hair, Elizabeth worked the skirt upward on her body. She tucked it up under her armpits, and it fit snugly around her chest.

When her hair was plaited and the skirt repositioned, the women pulled Elizabeth up and looked her over. They cackled and nodded, as if she was more acceptable. Her braids fell to the front of her shoulders, twisted at the end with strands of grass. Elizabeth felt a dread, not knowing what she was being prepared for. Then they led her to the low stone wall with the burned wood.

The visitors rode their horses and led the two ponies to the fire pit. The appearance of the three visiting Indians was different from any Elizabeth had seen. They looked in some ways like Indians, but in other ways, not. Their hair was cut short, cropped off even with their ears. They wore shirts with buttons. *Did they kill for those shirts?* Elizabeth wondered.

The visitors wore breeches, though Indian style breeches. Their legs were fully covered with leather leggings. Fringe trimmed the outside of the legs. Their shoes were the same as other Indian shoes, leather, but more heavily decorated than others Elizabeth had seen. The men had beads and shells woven onto their moccasins. *They dress like a white man but walk the Indian way,* Elizabeth thought to herself.

The old man with the long pipe in his hand was sitting on his stone like a king on his throne. He brought the pipe to his lips frequently. The women presented Elizabeth to the visitors, who dismounted and approached the fire pit.

The old man with the pipe still had a negative demeanor, and Elizabeth wondered what that meant. Elizabeth looked at the strangers. They conducted their own inspection of her, turning Elizabeth around and studying her closely. She was glad she had pulled the skirt up over her chest.

They all stood silent for what seemed too long. Then the men exchanged several short guttural phrases, and the man with the pipe gestured something that looked like approval. *Did he say "YES?"* The square women seemed pleased, but Elizabeth still had no idea what they intended to do with her.

## Traded for a Pot, a Knife and a Golden Pony—May 30th

After the inspection and the old man's apparent approval, one of the visitors took a bundle of leather from his horse. He unrolled it onto the ground and displayed three hefty knives. The blades glinted in the morning sun. The handles appeared to be made of bone.

Next to the knives another visiting Indian placed a large metal pot. As a final touch, he delicately lifted the wire handle as if to demonstrate that it was strong and movable. *The neighbors have brought gifts,* Elizabeth thought, *and probably quite a novelty.* She hadn't seen an actual cooking pot since she left the fort.

Then the third visiting Indian brought around the two ponies. The first was the color of honey, his golden coat shining in the morning sun. The second was a beautiful paint with gentle eyes and thick lashes. The tall Indian in the button shirt offered some throaty conversation, motioned to the ponies and then was quiet.

For the first time, the craggy old man's lips curled upward. His stained teeth revealed his approval, and he lifted his pipe in confirmation. He took the rope and led the golden pony to one of his warriors. Everyone else remained stoic while he touched the knives. He chose one and lifted it over his head to see the metal glimmer in the sun. Then he touched the movable handle of the cooking pot. When the handle swung to one side, he laughed, just like an Englishman.

Elizabeth was amused. *How strange we humans are, being so different, and yet in some ways we are just the very same.* As Elizabeth thought about the commonality of laughter, the square woman who had smiled at her handed her rope to one of the visitors in the leather britches. Then the Indian woman's face took on an expression of kindness.

The woman who smiled looked Elizabeth in the eye. She gently touched one of Elizabeth's braids and tucked it behind her shoulder. The woman put her hand on Elizabeth's cheek, following the curve of it. Then she turned away and went back to stand with her Indian sisters.

Before she had time to think about it, the visiting Indian led her away from the square women. Then she realized her fate. She was being traded for a pot, a knife and a golden pony.

The three Indians in their button shirts led Elizabeth by her rope to the side of the spotted pony. One warrior took charge of her and looked sternly into Elizabeth's eyes. He cupped his big hands and motioned for her to get up onto the horse. She tried to raise her arms to get onto the pony, but she couldn't. He seemed to understand and motioned to one of his companions.

Another brave went to the other side of the pony and held Elizabeth's hands over the horse's back. She placed a foot in the first brave's hands, and he boosted her up. She sat with one knee bent over the pony's back, just enough to keep her balance. The other leg dangled down the side of the horse. The two braves paused and checked her balance. She was astonished at their efforts to ensure she was secure.

In just a moment, with no more celebration, the business was over. The square women went back to their camp. The children went with their mothers to their tipis. The craggy old man sat down on his log, turning the knife in his hands.

The visiting braves mounted their horses and led Elizabeth's paint out of the camp, across the Neches River and up the opposite bank.

Elizabeth turned her back on the square people and wondered what waited for her ahead.

## Life with the Delaware — May 30th

The ponies walked through the forest in the shade of the tall pines. Elizabeth thought it was the most beautiful place she'd ever seen. The ground was a carpet of ancient leaves that silenced the pony hooves. Wild azaleas bowed their flowered arches between the trees, and they bobbed in the gentle breeze. The three men in long leather breeches made no aggression toward her, and the peace of the woods settled Elizabeth's soul.

They came to a village on the western edge of the Angelina River. The men dismounted. Without any help Elizabeth turned her belly to her little pony and slid down until her feet touched the ground. Her aching arms collapsed in front of her.

People of all ages scurried around. Elizabeth saw what looked like permanent homes. Their buildings were a dome construction. They were framed by branches and covered over with sections of birchbark peeled away from the trees. These were not the temporary tipis of the Comanches or the Kiowa. These homes were wig-wams, not so different from pioneer cabins. It was the home of people who stayed in one place a while.

These people were a band of Delaware Indians. The Delaware had been crowded out of their original lands after the American Revolution. They were farmers and fishermen, sustaining a good life along the rich delta of the Delaware River. They had always been a peaceful people, teaching their children to fish, hunt and garden. And for their agreeableness, they had always been cheated.

William Penn made trade with these folks long ago. His agreement seemed fair more than a century ago, but that deal was betrayed. When William died, his sons Thomas and John double-crossed the Delaware with something called the "Walking Purchase." Gradually, the Deleware were driven out of that region, so they sought out new rivers to sustain their culture.

Though they never lost the sting of their betrayal, they held to their goodness. They were peace loving. Elizabeth had no way to know at the time how fortunate she was to be in their care.

Women came and led her again with her leash, and then they tugged at Elizabeth to sit. They all sat together, and Elizabeth listened again to babble that made no sense to her.

The women sat in a circle with a large wooden bowl in the center. The bowl was full of beads the women were lacing. When they finished a string of blue-green beads they tied off the ends and put that string with others hanging on a trellis. There were strings of various seeds in red and yellow; there were strings of midnight blue beads. When Elizabeth joined them, they were all making strings of turquoise, lacing the beads onto several strands of hair from the tails of their horses.

They handed Elizabeth a strand of the horsetail hairs, three hairs twisted together. One woman demonstrated to her what was expected. Elizabeth followed her lead, stringing the beads as if she'd been doing it for years.

Children tossed sticks and played as they chased their dogs around the camp. When food was ready, they gave Elizabeth chunks of meat, just like their own. There was a pile of roasted corn, and when it was cool enough to touch the cobs were passed around. Elizabeth was treated as if she belonged.

But Elizabeth didn't belong. And that became clear in that she was passed from hut to hut. She became the guest of all the families in the village, as much servant as guest. She was shared around to do whatever needed doing and spent nights in all the huts. She wished more than ever to be back with her family so she would have something to call "home."

## Bad News — June 8th

"Hey, Ben. Chow time. Come on, let's go get some chow." Rowdy Daves slapped Benjamin Kellogg on his back with a glove. Rowdy and Benjamin had only been friends for three weeks, but the brotherhood was tight from their first introduction. The two were dock hands at the shipyards in Harrisburg, unloading all the fine things coming in to make a new republic.

Two brothers by name of Allen were investing heavily in the future of this muddy, burned-out wreck of a place. As it turned out in the years to come, their dreams would be fulfilled as the city of Houston emerged into one of the most important business centers in the world. But in 1836 it was a vision only the Allen brothers could see.

A bell rang out from two blocks away, indicating the noon hour. Ben waved off to the men on the ship to let them know it was time for a dinner break. The unloading would have to wait. A meal of hot soup and crusty bread would be waiting down in a giant shed the Allen brothers provided to their warehouse workers.

Rowdy was a good man to spend time with because he was a talker. He came from New Orleans and had seen a lot of interesting things, had a lot of stories to tell. Benjamin would rather listen than talk, so that worked out well. They were a comical pair — Rowdy a short, wiry animated man; Ben, hulking and quiet in comparison.

Today Rowdy had a newspaper in his back pocket. The two men went through the chow line, carried their food to a table, sat down and began to eat. About half-way through the meal Rowdy took the paper out of his pocket and laid it on the table. "I'm gettin' a drink. You want one, Ben?"

Ben nodded his head in acceptance. Rowdy went to one of the water barrels set out near the tables. The practice was to take the dipper hanging from the barrel, flip back the hinged opening in the top of the barrel, dip out your water into a tin cup from the stash in a wooden crate next to the barrel. When he finished drinking, a person simply threw his cup back in the stash. Very convenient, if not very sanitary. Rowdy brought back two cups of water. He put the cups on the table, sat down and flipped open his newspaper.

"Well, let's see what kind'a trouble we got now," he said laughing. Ben sat quietly finishing his meal. He took one of the tin cups, gave his friend a slight nod of thanks and drank while Rowdy read aloud.

"First page—look'a here! Elections gonna take place. Burnet don't want no part of it! I'd bet on Austin over Smith, but ol' Sam might decide to come into it before it's all over with. Then it'll be a toss-up, I guess. Austin or Houston. What do you think, Ben?"

Ben chewed, glanced over at the paper, nodded his head and took another bite of his bread.

Rowdy turned to page four of his four-page monthly. "Well, they done it again, those Injuns," he said with a smack in the corner of his mouth. "Looks like they took five this time." Ben heard what Rowdy said, and it concerned him only slightly. He began to calculate how long Elizabeth had been on the trail. Several weeks at least. Surely she was safely tucked away inside the twelve-foot walls of the family fortress by now. *Shouldn't be a worry*, he thought.

"They got the names here," Rowdy said. "They's Parker kids and a Plummer woman, and . . . ." Rowdy stopped reading. His face froze as if shot through with an arrow. He wished he hadn't read it out loud, but it was too late; he had already said it. He sat like a statue and moved only his eyes slowly toward his friend.

Ben was also sitting like a stone. He too wished Rowdy hadn't read those names aloud. He wouldn't have minded if they had been the names of some other people, but not those names. "Is that what it says?" Ben was stunned.

For the first time in his life, Rowdy Daves didn't know what to say. He looked back at the paper and then at Ben.

For several seconds Ben and Rowdy looked at each other. No one else in that crowded space could know the terrible communication they exchanged in that look, but Ben knew something dreadful was still on that paper.

Ben reached for the newspaper, but Rowdy kept it away, held it behind his back. He made his mouth form something like a smile, fighting off the horror in the question he knew he needed to ask his friend. For a man who had always held the entire house in the grasp of his entertaining ways, someone who had always, always known exactly what to say, Rowdy was at a loss. He knew he had to complete the report from the newspaper, but he also knew he was about to choke on the name he'd have to say. He searched for a way out of the truth, but he had to ask. He stammered, "Ben, what did you say was your wife's name?"

Ben was turned fully facing his friend. He knew it was more than one of his silly games that made Rowdy jerk the paper away. He had talked about his wife many times at work. He had told Rowdy that he planned to go find his wife at the Parker place and take her back to Gonzales. Rowdy knew Benjamin's plans. And he knew Ben's wife's name was Elizabeth.

Ben's face was growing red. He had a death grip on his tin cup. A ghostly transition began, as Ben leaned ever so gradually closer to Rowdy. Ben's presence grew bigger as the moments passed, and Rowdy knew he had to tell Ben the rest.

Rowdy leaned back, away from his overbearing friend. He pulled the newspaper around and handed it to Ben.

"Elizabeth," he said very quietly. The two men just looked at each other.

"Elizabeth Kellogg," Rowdy repeated the whisper as he handed the paper over. Ben felt those words cut through his heart on their way to his brain. Rowdy wondered if his friend would retaliate for the hurt he had inflicted.

Ben took the paper and turned it to page four. His eyes searched for the part that told about the raid. There it was, the whole story in its abbreviated form. The newspaper people couldn't convey the full impact of that event, but the skeleton of it was there. And the list of names was there. And that was really more than Benjamin Kellogg wanted to see.

Ben began to collapse, like one of the sails coming down on one of those ships down on the dock. The life-wind in him was evaporating.

Rowdy stood up and put a hand on his friend's big shoulder. Ben was shaking. Rowdy motioned to one of the other men at the table. "We got a sick man here," he said. "We need to get him some help."

The only help available for sickness was the company infirmary. His friends helped him to the infirmary where he stayed overnight. Ben's sickness was desperation, and there was no medication for that.

The women who attended the sick listened to his story. He cried and agonized over what he knew and what he didn't know. In his sleeplessness he reached into his pocket and fondled the heavy gold coin Elizabeth had given him on their last night together. He looked into the sky and wondered if dead sons and daughters can look down from heaven and see what goes on back on earth. Then he decided that tomorrow he would go back to work until he could think clear enough to do something else.

## Final Camp — Three Full Moons

The Delaware people of the bark wig-wams were partners with nature. They had always embraced new knowledge. At one time they sent a request to the United States asking for a teacher and someone to help them speak English. They were sociable and inclusive. In her earliest days with them, they included Elizabeth in all their work. They took her to their gardens, and they included her in the women's working circles to string their beads. Elizabeth had always been a good worker, and she welcomed the opportunity for something purposeful to do with her hands.

For weeks she spent her days with the women. Elizabeth did what she had done all her life, carrying water, weeding the garden rows, picking the vegetables, shucking the corn, cleaning the beans. Now she easily learned to lace the beads. *They're not so different from me*, she thought, but she still longed to go back to her people.

Her shoulders ached and shot pain into her back. Every day she tried to lift her arms a little higher. Gradually she improved her abilities to function, but always with the pain.

Elizabeth estimated from her time-keeping that she had come to the wig-wams approximately the first part of June. The weather agreed with her estimation. The heat increased, and the days were longer. Judging from the maturity of the crops she was confident that it was summer.

She knew she had walked a long way from the church people at the fortress. She believed the forest around the bark huts was a long way from Harrisburg. So she paid attention to the other things in nature to estimate where she was and how long she had been in captivity.

She had been lonely, afraid and in pain with the other Indians. Now she felt she could relate to the wig-wam people as being more like herself, and she wasn't afraid. They treated her with some regard. She began to talk. Of course, no one understood her, but she said what was on her mind as if they could.

"Look at these beautiful beans!" she said in the garden one day. The woman near her looked surprised and turned her attention to the flower where Elizabeth pointed. Elizabeth knew she didn't understand a word.

Elizabeth danced across the garden a few rows away, while the women and children stood looking at her. "And look at this young corn!" she said as she turned to them, stood tall and put her hands on her hips.

"You brought me out here to work, didn't you?" she continued talking in English to her stunned audience. "Well, let's get busy!" she said as she flopped down and began to pull weeds.

The Indian women and children stood looking at Elizabeth, and she pretended to ignore them. She began to sing some hymns she remembered from her days worshiping with those Baptist Parkers. She wondered if she was losing her mind, or if her pretense was a healthy coping game. "No matter," she said aloud to no one in particular. "Getting prairie madness is better than being dead, so you just listen to me tell you what I think!"

Slowly the Indian women and children accepted her chatter. They worked all the time, going out in teams to gather vegetation. They strung the beads, they pulled the weeds and carried water to the vegetable crops. When that was done, they cleaned the pelts and softened the leather from the animals the men brought in. While she helped them, Elizabeth talked to herself and to her captors as if they understood. It gave her enough peace of mind to make it through the weeks.

"I watch the moon, you know," she said one evening. It was after their evening gathering near the campfire. The adults were reclining, and the children threw sticks for their dogs to chase. "The moon tells me how long I've been with you people," she continued. "It's been approximately ten weeks!" She looked around her. A few children were watching her, but no one else paid her any mind. "Yes, ma'am, the night before we arrived was a full moon. And tonight is the third full moon. That has to be at least ten weeks, maybe more."

Being ignored except for the work she could contribute made her remember that she used to enjoy anonymity. But this way of being "dismissed" from life was more painful than being "on show."

"Ten weeks is a long time," she said more quietly. "I wish you could tell me how long I have to stay here." Her voice wasn't much more than a whisper as tears flooded her eyes. "The moon will change, and someone will come to get me," she said louder in defiance, determined not to completely break.

A little girl stopped chasing her dog and looked in Elizabeth's face. Elizabeth sniffed her desperation away, bent low and growled, "I used to be a little girl, you know!" She squinted her eyes and continued to reassure herself, "and there ARE people who love me!" The child's eyes grew big, and she ran away.

Talking to herself about the moon helped. She began to look up there and talk to those she loved who had gone to their after-life. "Sydnie," she said to her daughter-in-law, "Sydnie, can you see me? I remember you." And she talked to her son. "John Benjamin, do you see Texas now? Do you know what Sam Houston did after the Alamo?" She waited and thought it all over. So much had happened to Texas since they first arrived in Mexico.

Then she remembered her mama. When the memories of the blood and the Indian yelping came back, she had to stop remembering. She looked around at the Delaware people and was at least thankful not to be hanging in a tree at night.

She talked to her grandson. "Little John-Boy, are you growing up?" She asked the sky. "Can you see that moon from Gonzales?"

Then a night came when there was no moon. The sky was black. That in itself didn't get Elizabeth's attention, because that happened every month. But that night a bolt of lightning split the sky. A flock of birds was roosting in a tree on the edge of the village, and as the jagged electricity from heaven crackled, hundreds of birds flew from their branches. At first, they flew low, almost touching the ground. Everyone in the camp crouched down and ducked their heads. Then the flock took a higher flight path, and they were gone.

The men stood together in silence and looked to the sky. From the light of the fire Elizabeth saw them suddenly all go into their huts and go to sleep for the night. The next morning, everything changed.

On the morning after the lightning, the women got up early, but they didn't go to the gardens. Elizabeth thought they were on their way there, but instead she was taken to the center of the village.

The women collected all the beaded strands from the trellis. They rolled them carefully, put them in pouches tied with leather straps and gave them to one of the braves. He pulled the leather straps tight and carefully hung the pouches around his neck.

Another team of women folded the fur pelts they had cleaned and softened. With similar long leather straps they tied the pelts and strapped them across the back of a pony.

Two braves brought their horses around leading a familiar little painted pony. A warrior bent down and put out his hand. He motioned for Elizabeth to get up on the little horse. She struggled again with her arms and he helped her. A trading group was organized. Elizabeth could tell the beads and the furs were to be sold, and she was part of the inventory. In a short time, she was led out of the camp riding the same pony she rode in on.

## Keeping a Promise — July 10th

On a day in July, the docks in Harrisburg were as hot as coals in a Saturday night fire. The foreman approached Benjamin Kellogg. "Somebody here to see you," he said.

Benjamin felt feverish, had a terrible cough, and he welcomed the break. He waved off the men on the ship and alerted his friend Rowdy Daves that he was stepping away from their work. He followed the foreman to the warehouse, coughing all the way. They went to the offices set up for the shipping company.

Tom and Chico were taking Charlotte back to New Orleans where Anthony Mexia waited for her. Harrisburg was right in their path. Tom had asked around the docks if a Ben Kellogg was known. As it happened, Ben Kellogg and Rowdy Daves were well known because of Rowdy's antics when the men came to get their work assignments or collect their pay. Ben was easy to find.

As he entered the door, Ben saw Tom's familiar, clean-shaven face. The two men shook hands. Tom wrapped both hands around Ben's hand and held the grip longer than he had to. He searched Ben's eyes to assess how much he might already know.

"I had to come," Tom said. He waited for Ben to say something... anything to let Tom know where to start with his account.

"I'm really glad you did," Ben said. "What do you know?" he asked in between coughs.

Ben reached into his pocket and brought out a section of sugar cane. It was one of the remedies used around the docks to keep the coughing down. "Let's go sit down outside," Tom said as Benjamin took a chew of the cane.

Ben rolled the bite of cane around in his mouth, and it settled his cough some. They walked out and found a bench in front of a warehouse.

"Did you hear about the raid?" Tom asked, hoping the answer would be yes. He didn't want to give that terrible news. He looked forward to sharing what little hope he could offer his friend.

Ben sat with his elbows on his thighs, hands clamped together holding the rest of the cane and spit out the bite he had in his mouth. He leaned forward and shook his head as he struggled to tell Tom what he had read in the paper last month. "That's all I know," he said as he cleared another cough from his throat. "I've been sick with worry, but where could I go? What could I do? I wouldn't know where to start." He looked at Tom and took another chew. He really wanted to get some idea of anything he might do to find out where Elizabeth was and what she was going through, to get her back if possible.

"I went over there," Tom said. "The day I went your brother-in-law was there with about a dozen others, gathering up bones and taking care of the stock."

"Who did they kill? Do you know who they killed?"

"I don't know, Ben. That was a lot of people out there, and I didn't know them. I'm sorry, that's all I can tell you. But they told me your brother-in-law is going to make up a ranging company and go get the family back."

Ben nodded his head, wondering which Parker had taken on this task. "Who is that," he asked. "Which one?"

"James," Tom said. "They told me James had taken it up. It was his daughter, you know, and his grandson. And some children from another family."

Ben hung his head. "Rachael. That was her favorite niece. She used to play with our boy, John." Ben closed his eyes forcing control of the tension he felt. He wanted to hit something hard, but he knew it wouldn't bring Elizabeth back. "I shouldn't have let her go. I should have taken her to Gonzales."

"I'm sorry, Ben. I wish I had better news for you. But I can tell you she was happy to get there. We stayed overnight, and the whole family was celebrating. I don't know how long she had before this happened, but I know she was happy when she got there," Tom told him.

Ben lifted his head and nodded to Tom. "If you hear anything more, if you come through here again, just find out what you can. I'll keep working till I know anything more." Ben began to cough again, and he struggled for his breath.

"We're on our way to New Orleans. News comes through there but might get here first. I might be back through here before winter. I'll check with these people when we come through." Tom motioned to the office space where they met. "If you're still here, I'll find you."

"Can't thank you enough," Ben said. "It's a help to know somebody is looking for her." He leaned back against the wall and looked into the sky. "God only knows what she's going through," he finished with a deep sigh.

"Miss Charlotte asked me to give you her regards," Tom said. "She sure thinks the world of Elizabeth."

Ben nodded.

Tom reached out to shake his hand goodbye. "I'll be goin' now."

The two men took a long look at each other, and then Tom turned to go. Ben watched him walk away. He remembered the day Tom had promised to take care of Elizabeth, and Ben knew in Texas that was a promise no one could have kept.

# Nacogdoches — August 19th

"Na-ko-do-che."

Elizabeth overheard a word that sounded like a town she knew was in far east Texas. Nacogdoches. It was an important village, venerated as far back as anyone could remember.

According to legend, long ago an Indian chief living on the Sabine River had twin sons. He sent them in opposite directions, one east and one west. After three days' journey, each son stopped and built his village. The dark-haired son went east and built Natchitoches in what was destined to become part of Louisiana. The blond-haired twin went west and built Nacogdoches, destined to become a trading mecca in Tejas, coveted by the French, Spanish, Mexicans and Anglo-Texians. "Nacogdoches" was a familiar word by 1836. The village was a place of legends, and it was well known for the Indian swapping that went on there.

As they came into the village, the warriors seemed to know exactly where to go. This was not their first visit. They went without hesitation to the trading post.

The Indians got down from their ponies and tied them securely to a Cypress cross beam. Elizabeth's leather wrap had a six-inch tether hanging from each side, and one of the warriors kept a hand on her at all times. They all walked into the trading post.

Elizabeth saw stacks of hides, cooking pots and pans of all sizes, tools for gardening and hardware she recognized as part of a water pump. There were muskets stacked in a box and supplies of musket balls, gun powder and wads nearby.

The little room was full of men. Two were leaning on the counter next to a huge black cash register talking to the shopkeeper. Four others were sitting at a table playing cards. Elizabeth heard English and Spanish. Then they all went quiet.

The shopkeeper's eyes went wide, and he began to stammer. The others looked at Elizabeth, looked her up and down, but no one talked to her.

The tallest brave walked ahead with the bags of beads. He stopped a few yards from Elizabeth and her guard. The two men at the counter turned around, and the shopkeeper rushed over. He spit out some of their Indian language, shaking his head and grinning as if he was embarrassed over his clumsiness. The shopkeeper stuttered and fidgeted. They carried on a fractured conversation with a lot of hand gestures.

The brave removed the bags of beads from his shoulders. "Uuuum-mm," he grunted toward the two men standing by the cash register. He placed the beads on the counter as the two men stepped away. The storekeeper looked at the beads but didn't seem impressed. They exchanged some more Indian words, and the shopkeeper glanced several times at Elizabeth. The tall warrior gestured to the door, and the two of them went to see the buffalo hides, while Elizabeth waited inside with the second Indian. It was agonizing for Elizabeth to stand there in the presence of the white men looking at her. She tightened her lips, squared her shoulders, and glared at the pots and pans.

The white man and the Indian returned. More words were exchanged. It seemed the beads and buffalo hides were not interesting, and then the conversation shifted to Elizabeth.

"This woman," the white man said as he shook his jittery hands. He continued in his Indian talk. Most of it she couldn't understand, but from what she heard she knew she was to be sold, and the Indians wanted one hundred fifty American dollars for her.

"I need to go get the money," he said. He looked at Elizabeth. She thought most of what he was saying in English was for her benefit, and she was grateful. He told the Indians to wait.

The shopkeeper knew something no one else in the room knew. He knew James Parker. And he knew James had arrived in Nacogdoches just yesterday, trying to convince Sam Houston to fund a ranging troop. The ranging troop was needed to search for white women and children taken recently by Indians. And he knew Elizabeth was one of those women.

Elizabeth was hopeful and humiliated all at the same time. While she had never in her life imagined that she would be "sold," she preferred being sold to being captive, if she might at least become the property of white people. And enduring humiliation one more time would be part of her cost.

## The Trading Post — August 19th

Indians are patient people.

Two Delaware braves sat in front of the trading post in Nacogdoches, Texas, facing opposite directions. The sun was in the west, and they enjoyed the afternoon shade. Elizabeth sat between them, facing the street. Each man had a discreet grip on the leather tail hanging from the sides of the leather skirt Elizabeth had pulled up over her chest. They were going to make sure she was under their control.

Could she run? The temptation was great, but as she thought about it, she imagined what could happen then. How far would she get? Would someone come to her rescue? Would there be gunfire? She rationalized they were about to give her up anyway, so she convinced herself to wait.

The Delaware band on the Angelina River had treated Elizabeth well. These were the last stragglers trying to survive despite their eviction time after time, place after place. They had gradually acculturated. More than any other people Elizabeth knew, the Delaware were trying to accept immigration and still maintain their own cultural dignity.

Elizabeth saw the man from the trading post and two others coming up the street, heading their way. Elizabeth felt her heart pounding. One of the men looked like her brother-in-law, James Parker. He was the Parker she trusted the least, but today he was a welcome sight. The three men walked up to the Indians.

"Elizabeth?"

"Yes, James. It's me," she said. She hadn't heard English in months. Her name sounded like music as he said it.

James reached for her hands and noticed how scarred and swollen they were. She stood, and the Indians stood. They flicked his hands away from her to make it clear—she was not free to go. Not without some money.

"Oh, Elizabeth, I'm so glad to see you. We're going to take you home. I just have to get the money."

"I understand," she said.

He gestured to the man from the trading post. "Will'm can tell these Indians not to leave town. You'll have to stay with them. I'll be back tomorrow with the money. I have a plan. You just have faith, and we'll get you home."

"Please, James. Please, take me with you. How much money do you need? I left money with Mama. Maybe we can find Benjamin in Harrisburg, he has money," she pleaded.

James took off his hat and held it in both hands in front of him as she made her case. He shifted his stance from one foot to another. "I don't know how you can do it, James, but please, please take me with you." Elizabeth was desperate.

"Elizabeth, I know how important this is." He looked at the tallest Indian whose eyes were squinted and whose brows were furrowed.

James turned to his side and tried to speak only to Elizabeth. "I came here to appeal to Old Sam for help," he explained. "After the fort was attacked, I knew we had to get more help. I've been doggin' Sam's trail, pleading with him for more Rangers, Elizabeth."

"Take me with you to General Houston," she said. She tried to step toward him, but the braves wouldn't let her go. The braves frowned and pushed James away. They made a gesture with their hands, as if he should cross their palms with money before they would let Elizabeth go.

James turned again to the man from the trading post. "Will'm, you talk to 'em. Tell them not to leave." James instructed. The man from the general store spoke in the Indian way and relayed James' message.

"Uummm," the tallest Indian responded with a nod of his head.

"Ask them if they will stay for the money. Tell them if they go away, I can't bring them money." James looked at the Indians. "I'll put them up for the night and bring them food. I'll meet them here in the morning. Right here. Tell them, Will'm. And ask if they'll agree."

The interpreter spoke again. The Indians talked together and then made some arm gestures. The man who spoke Indian said to James, "until the sun goes down tomorrow. You have that long."

"That's long enough," James said, looking sternly into the eyes of the tallest warrior.

James arranged for a single room in a nearby boarding house. The room was empty except for one straight chair. He motioned for them to go in, and he closed the door. He stabled the Indian ponies in the town livery and made sure they were secured for the night.

"Go get them some grub from that cantina," James said to the man named Will'm. "I'll stay here till you get back. Then you stay here to-night while I work with Sam."

The Indians sat cross-legged on the floor, just as they would back in their camp. One sat in front of the door, the other across the room looking at the door.

"One more night," Elizabeth thought. "I can do this for one more night." And she spent the night sitting in the straight chair, listening to their snores.

# Part Five:
# Journey to Freedom

# Paying a Bounty — August 20th

On the morning of August 20, 1836, Sam Houston awoke early. His first task of the day was to complete a document of release noting the legal, fair, compassionate, ethical and friendly exchange of one hundred fifty dollars in gold for the woman Elizabeth Kellogg. He knew James Parker would be there early to collect the gold and go to claim the first of his relatives to be ransomed after the awful, awful raid the previous May.

Old Sam had a rented space in town. He was still recovering from a leg wound taken at San Jacinto. He had defeated Santa Anna, taken him captive, redeemed his precious Texas and earned respect throughout the new Republic. His heart was full. He didn't need much more.

Within the walls of his space was his bed, a desk, two heavy chairs and a large safe. Within the safe was a treasure trove of documents, both legal and potentially legal. But today, the most important thing in his vault was gold. Alone in the early morning he carefully turned the dial until it touched all the secret numbers. He heard the clicks, turned the bolt and opened the door.

*A ransom for her life*, he thought to himself. *There is no other way. And it is money well spent.*

Sam Houston had many, many goals. With his recent victory at the San Jacinto River, he believed anything was possible. He defeated the self-described "Napoleon of the West." He was being urged to run for president in the coming election. He was bent on an alliance with the Indian nations, and he believed they could all live together in peace. Today's ransom was a step in the direction toward all his goals.

In the corner of his multi-functional room, he found a small leather pouch someone had used to carry gunpowder. Sam rubbed the leather between his fingers, trying to remember who left it behind. It shouldn't matter. It was the perfect way to secure the coins. In they went, and the drawstring was pulled tight. Then he sat at his desk and propped his wounded leg up on the other chair.

Paper was a rare and precious commodity in the pioneer settlements, and what was available was used judiciously. It was intended for only the most honorable, significant, urgent recordings. Letters back home, pledges of intent to marry, agreements for loans, commitments of debts, and sometimes treaties among groups of people. Sam pulled open the bottom drawer of his big desk and drew out a deep box. Carefully he opened that box and slid out the second page from the top. With equal care he slid the top page back in place. That cover page would protect the rest of the pages for future use. He closed the box and returned it to the bottom drawer.

He took a new goose quill with a fine, strong point from a porcelain tray on the top of the desk. From another drawer, he took a tiny bottle of black ink. As he opened the bottle, he leaned back and thought about what he wanted to write. He reached over to a side shelf and poured himself some whiskey.

The paper needed to be respectful to everyone. It was meant to be a statement of trust. It wasn't even a required document, but in Sam's experience it was always, always good to have a record of a good deed. He was especially scrupulous when dealing with Indians. He wrote what he thought best and put the paper under the leather pouch. Just as he finished, James Parker knocked on the open door to Sam's room.

"Come on in here, James," Sam Houston shouted from his chair. "Look here, what I've got. It's a document to memorialize this day and what you've done. Look it over and see what you think." He reached for the whiskey and drank while James read.

"I think we have to do whatever we can to stop the Indians, Sam. I know you said you can't give me Rangers." James read the paper. "At least Elizabeth will get back home. I'm obliged to you for this." He put the paper back down on the desk.

The paper had a lot of blank space. The recording was simple and succinct. "Sam Houston gives James Parker $150.00 in gold to be paid to the Delaware Indians as ransom for his sister-in-law, Elizabeth Kellogg, on this twentieth day of August, 1836, in the town of Nacogdoches, the Republic of Texas." Then there was a line for James Parker to write his name.

Sam spoke from his chair. "We have to meet them on their terms, James. If we can at least find a way with the friendlies, that's a start. I know you've been wanting help. I'll do all I can, but we have to work with them. And I just don't have the money for those Rangers you want. At least in this situation everyone comes out whole. Take this, and let's move forward." Sam pushed the leather bag of gold in James' direction.

James took the paper and bent over at Sam Houston's big desk. He picked up the quill and signed his name. "This is a start. I agree. After I get her back home, I'll be back to see you."

Sam Houston dipped his head and looked at James out of the corner of his eye. Sam was a man who made things work. With the Republic in its infancy he had a lot on his mind. Getting a white woman home was a brief distraction but an important one. He hoped James would just sign the paper, take the gold and move on.

James slid the signed paper across the desk, and Sam looked at the signature. "I'll keep this in the vault, James. It'll be the best reference we can have. It sets a precedent. Now, you take this gold and get that woman back home." He smiled and tossed the little leather bag to James.

James snagged up the little bag, tossed it up just a fraction and tucked it into his pocket. Then he did as Sam had wished and walked away to complete the ransom. He didn't even consider counting it. If Sam gave it to him, he knew it was right.

James walked across the street and down the block to where the Indians were waiting in front of the trading post. The language difference was always a problem, but the Delaware seemed able to understand enough to get them through their trading deals. Today would be no different.

The two Indians and Elizabeth were standing in a row, shoulder-to-shoulder on the front stoop of the place. Elizabeth's heart was pounding as she saw her brother-in-law approaching. She took a deep breath and looked at her captors.

James approached the group and stopped in front of them. Elizabeth was in the center, with a Delaware brave on each side of her. James slowly held out the bag of gold coins. He took out a small one and held it up between two fingers, displaying it to communicate his intention. Then he shook the little bag. The coins clanked inside. The Indians looked at each other.

One of the men spoke to the other in their language. Elizabeth took another breath and leaned forward to test her freedom. Yes, it was true. She took a step and the Indians let her. Then the warrior held out his arm in front of her. He put his palm flat in front of James. The single coin was returned to the bag, and the small pouch of leather was then placed on his waiting palm. The Indian smiled, and he pushed Elizabeth forward.

"Step away slowly," James told her, and she did. She wanted to breathe, but she was afraid to. Two steps, then another. "Stop," James said.

The Indians were looking into the bag. Their heads were bent together, counting the coins and talking in their guttural, halting language. Finally, the man who took the pouch looked at James and gave something like a salute. Then they turned and walked away.

## Walking Away — August 20th

Elizabeth's head was swimming with optimism. She had often wondered how this moment would feel. She talked herself through each step. She half believed they would come back and take her away again.

*If I can only get inside a real building without them, I'll be safe*, she thought.

There was a lot of shame that returned with all women after they were taken captive. Elizabeth knew that. She felt the weight of their imaginations about her experiences as she walked through the street with people staring.

It had become part of the culture of Tejas. The men had come for the land, for adventure, to leave their past behind and have a better future. Elizabeth wasn't the first woman to pay for all that with her dignity.

A group of men were standing on the boardwalk outside the doorway of Sam Houston's office building. Elizabeth knew she was "on show" as she walked in her leather skirt pulled up to her arm pits. *This can't be any worse than the raid,* she told herself. Despite her humiliation she squared her shoulders, lifted her chin just a little and ignored them.

James had arranged for a room where Elizabeth could stay, in the same boarding house where she had stayed with the Indians the night before. Without any conversation he led her straight to the room. They went inside, and he closed the door behind them.

James took off his hat. Elizabeth looked around the room. This room was furnished. There was a single bed with a small table on one side and a straight wooden chair on the other. A large white basin sat on the table, and a fat pitcher of water sat inside the basin. A clean, soft cloth was folded and tucked into the handle of the pitcher.

The bed was made with a thick quilt and a puffy pillow. A pair of black leather shoes sat near the little table, ladies' shoes with little heels and a hard sole. A pair of freshly washed cotton stockings were tucked inside the high tops of the shoes.

Laying across the bed was a dress. It was beautiful. White background with green and purple flowers. It had a double flounce collar with crocheted lace trim. The sleeves would fall just below her elbows and had a flounce that matched the collar. The neck was high, and the buttons connected in the front. There was a wide sash to tie in the back. The skirt flowed to her ankles.

"I hope this suits you," James said respectfully.

Elizabeth was so overcome she couldn't respond.

James lowered his head and spoke humbly. "I'll get you to Montgomery, 'Lizabeth. We'll leave tomorrow. Patsey will be thrilled to see you. Do you know anything about Rachael and the others?"

"No, James, I don't know anything. They separated us," she said as she looked around the room.

"I understand," he said. "Well... you... you make yourself comfortable. I'll be back later with some food."

She looked at her brother-in-law. She struggled to believe what was happening to her. She couldn't know how hard James had worked to achieve this rescue and how fortunate she was he accomplished it.

Seldom were women rescued so quickly. The timing of James' arrival in Nacogdoches, his friendship with Will'm at the trading post, and the Delaware's decision to trade Elizabeth on the 20th day of August was a fortuitous blending of events. No one could have planned it better.

After James left, Elizabeth stood in her room, astonished, wondering what would happen tomorrow.

She poured a small pool of the water into the basin and sat the pitcher on the floor. She dipped the cloth into the water and began to wipe her face. As she wiped her arms and legs, she realized how scratched and bruised she was. She noticed some of the scratches had already turned to scars, never to be wiped away. There was no looking glass in the room, but she knew she was not the same woman she had been the last day she was with her family. She wanted to unbraid her hair, but she knew she couldn't manage re-styling it.

When she felt adequately washed, she took the dress in her hands and pulled it to her face. It felt soft and smelled fresh. She struggled with the limitations of her arms but managed to slip it over her head. She cried. She had lots of reasons to cry. It was certainly for the joy of the dress and the reality that she was finally, truly liberated.

Her tears were partly from humiliation, realizing the shame she carried. It was partly from exhaustion and partly just in ecstatic anticipation of what would come next. She didn't know what she would say to her husband or what his reaction would be to her return. But in spite of all else, she knew this was the beginning of her journey home. She cried it all out, and then she washed her face again.

Late in the afternoon, James tapped on her door. "Hungry?" he asked.

Without words, she nodded. Yes. She was hungry. Suddenly she was very hungry. He widened the door, and there stood two women she didn't know. They had dishes covered with tea towels.

"These here are some ladies from the church, Elizabeth. They come to help us."

She moved aside and let them into her room. They put the dishes down on the small bed.

"Thank you." When the words came out of Elizabeth's mouth, they seemed foreign. It had been so very long since she had spoken her language to someone who could understand.

"Bless you." One of the women took Elizabeth's hands and held them. The woman felt warm, and she looked into Elizabeth's eyes with compassion. Elizabeth felt tears welling up in her own eyes, but she stiffened and refused to be weak. The woman let her go and stepped away.

The other woman patted Elizabeth on her shoulder. "We fried you some chicken," she said.

"Thank you, ladies," James said as he ushered them to the door.

"Please eat, Elizabeth, and get a good night sleep. We're leaving tomorrow, and you need your strength." Then he closed the door and was gone.

Elizabeth did eat. She took tiny bites, to savor each one in the safety of her room alone. She bent over to pull back the covers on her bed. Her window faced the west, and the early evening sun shone golden on the streets outside.

Elizabeth kneeled on the bed and looked outside at the ancient village of Nacogdoches. She thought about all she had seen. From Missouri to Illinois to Texas, from her Daddy's farm to the Parkers' church, to the fort, then to Gonzales, to the Sabine, and then back to her family by way of Harrisburg. She had met so many people along the way, and yet here she was alone. What was a life for, she wondered? Then she remembered her husband, Benjamin, and the littlest John Benjamin waiting in Gonzales. That was all she wanted now, to get back to them.

Elizabeth sat on the bed. As she turned and slipped her tired legs between the clean sheets, the calloused skin of her feet snagged the fabric. She closed her eyes to take in the freshness of it. Slowly she lowered herself onto the bed and settled the pillow under her neck. She purposely delayed the process, wanting every cell to enjoy the experience. She couldn't remember ever another day in her life when rest was so perfect. She snuggled under the covers and was soon asleep.

## Leaving Nacogdoches — August 21st

On the morning of August 21st, James Parker knocked on the door where Elizabeth spent her first night of freedom from the Indians. She had been awake for at least an hour. The smell of coffee came from somewhere, but she drank water from the pitcher in her room. James was in a hurry to leave, so there was no breakfast. That was fine with Elizabeth. Going home was better than eating breakfast.

James had recruited a two-man posse to accompany them in case of trouble. The two were independent rangers, sometimes on their own missions, sometimes on a mission for others. They were old acquaintances of James', typical of the rovers in those lawless days.

One man named Milligan had a distinctive head of long black hair streaked with white. Just over his right ear he had a wide patch of white hair that seemed wiry and out of control. James called him "Milly."

James called the other man "Shag." Shag had no hair at all, not a sprig on him anywhere to be seen. His head was slick as a stone. His face had no brows, no lashes, no beard. His skin was dark. His face was thin, and he had high cheek bones. Shag dressed like a white man, but in some ways, he resembled her captors too much for Elizabeth to be comfortable with him.

"Milly has a place back in Montgomery," James told Elizabeth. "He'll be glad for the company when we ride. He has as much reason to get back as we do."

"And Shag?" she asked.

James hesitated. He looked around like he was thinking of an answer. "Shag is really a good man to have around in case of trouble, Elizabeth. He's fine." She suspected outlaw tendencies, but if he helped her get home, she wouldn't count that against him.

James changed the subject. "Can you ride?" he asked her.

"I'm sure I can," she said. "But I need help getting on." She thought, *Even if I never had before I'd sure ride today.* She had ridden, maybe ten times years ago, before those pony rides with the Indians. It wasn't a skill she had perfected, but that wasn't going to stop her now.

She strained her leg upward toward the stirrup, but the horse moved in a circle. James held the reins and Milly stood on the opposite side of the horse. Finally, Elizabeth was able to secure her foot into the wooden stirrup, and the men helped her get one leg over. She settled into the saddle, this time with a leg on either side of the horse. She tucked her skirt around her and felt excitement stab into her. She was with people who spoke her language, and she was going home.

James handed her a "gut bag" full of water. Then he added a bundle of beef jerky strips crammed into a similar bag of leather. "This is all for the day," he said. "We'll loop these straps around the horn here, and it'll stay 'til you want it."

James worked with the food supplies to be sure they were secure. Then he packed a rolled blanket in the back of Elizabeth's saddle. He doubled-checked everything, and then he turned to his companions.

"Saddle up, Milly, let's head out," James said. Shag had been in his saddle a while, and his horse pranced impatiently.

Milligan pulled his long hair back out of his face and pushed it down with a leather hat as he mounted his horse. James got into his saddle and waved his gloved hand to the sky.

Just as daylight was showing strong through the pine trees, Milligan, Shag and James led Elizabeth out of Nacogdoches, beginning a long trip back to her family. They were bound for Montgomery, where James' wife, Patsey, would help Elizabeth fit back into society.

## Prairie Justice — August 23rd – 24th

The trail meant camping again, but Elizabeth was accustomed to that. They rode to the southwest, into the afternoon sun. The days were long in

August, and they rode late. It was evening before they stopped. They were traveling a well-worn trail, and they came upon a camp in the woods.

"Hey there neighbor," a man stepped out of the thick woods and hailed James and his party. "Where you headed?"

"We're going south, down to Montgomery. Just need a stop for the night," James said.

"Better stop here with us then. I'm Smith and this is my hand, Buck." He gestured to his companion back at the fire. "This is my land, and I'd be proud to have you camp here tonight."

"Thank you, Smith. I think we will," James said looking back at Milligan. "Always better to have more folks in a camp."

Everyone dismounted, and the men went to the fire. Elizabeth stayed back until James came to get her. "I'll make you a place to sleep, 'Lizbeth. No one will bother you."

"Yes, James. Thank you," she said, and she stood with her hands behind her back.

He unrolled her blanket and covered a space on the ground. "You make yourself comfortable, and I'll bring you some food." Elizabeth settled down on the blankets and took off her shoes. She sat cross-legged with her skirt covering her legs. She could feel a wave of peace coming over her, even though she knew there were many miles left to go before she would truly be home again. The smell of food was amazing.

"Here you go. Try this now." Elizabeth took a warm cup in her hands. James smiled at her and turned away. She drank the broth and found a chunk of meat in the cup. As she rolled the meat on her tongue, she could hear the men's conversation.

"Good thing ya'll stopped when you did," Smith said. He leaned against a crooked tree limb as he went on. "I been here two days. My ranch is just beyond that stand of trees, there. We been having In'jun troubles, and I went out looking for 'em. Stole my horses just a few days ago. But I found 'em." He chewed some and spit out a bit of bone. "I left two for dead, just back in the brush there." He paused and pointed a knife blade into the dark.

Elizabeth chewed slowly and thought about what might be lurking in the darkness. When she could see the bottom of the tin cup she got up and pulled her bedding a little closer to the fire.

"More stew here, ma'am." the rancher said. He removed his hat and approached her. "I go by Kyle, ma'am. My wife back in the cabin there, she shore would be pleased with a visit." He drew the rim of his hat in his hands and thought about his words. "Women out here, they just so rare. I hope you pass the night comfortable."

"Thank you, I'll take some more stew if you don't mind." She inched the bedding just a little closer, trying to get as much as possible into the protection of the men without being too close. James refilled her cup. "I don't know if we have time to meet, but tell your wife I wish her well."

Eating proper food and listening to English again was a comfort. Elizabeth felt a mental swirl, trying to accept her good fortune to be rescued. She knew it didn't always happen for captives and especially so soon after their seizure. She wanted to be as quiet and discreet as possible, just praying all the while that every step was taking them closer to Montgomery.

She returned her cup to the pile of utensils and pots collecting near the fire, went to her bedding and settled in. She didn't fall asleep so soon that night, but as she lay awake, she thought of many things for which she was thankful. She noticed that Shag took the guard for the night.

On the morning of August 24th, Kyle Smith was toasting flatbread and boiling coffee even before the sun was up. The aroma awakened Elizabeth, and she opened her eyes to see the twinkling of the last stars. She waited to hear the others and realized the rancher was packing his horses. Today they would all move out.

James rolled over on his bedroll and sat up. "You 'bout ready to travel on?" he asked Elizabeth.

"Sure, James. Soon as you say so." Elizabeth saw Shag standing in the same place she last saw him the night before. "Did he sleep at all?" she asked James.

James ignored her question and just laughed with a shake of his head. "Have some coffee, and we'll pack up. We'll leave soon as the sun is up."

With the coffee down and the horses packed, the party moved out. "I'll go with you as far as my place, and we'll be sure to get through that pass where I met up with those redskins," Smith said. He and Buck led the way with James and Elizabeth next in line. Milly and Shag brought up the rear.

The woods of east Texas thickened. Smith led them through a pass and pointed to a clearing.

"This was the place; just around there . . . Look, there's one . . ." The rancher spoke quietly and pointed to a body lying on the ground. It was bulging and gave off the putrid smell of death.

Milly, James and Elizabeth got down to take a close look. Smith, Buck and Shag stayed on their horses.

Elizabeth gasped. "That's him!" she said. James turned to look at her. She went nearer the body, held her hand to her nose and stared at the body.

The Indian was lying on his side in a contortion that left his arms over his head. The back of his upper arms was clearly visible. They had distinct red and black marks, jagged lines all the way around. One leg was bent at the knee, and he wore soft leather moccasins with tall leggings that came almost to his knee. Sewn onto the top of the leggings was a scalp pelt, silver gray, the same scalp pelt the Indian had taken from the Elder John Parker. She knew it was the same because those were the same markings on the arms that carried the scalp when he tied her hands.

"He's the one, James," she said without taking her eyes off the Indian. "That's your daddy's scalp around his leg. Those lines on his arms, I'd know those marks anywhere."

James was not really surprised to know the same Indians were this far east. He knew she was right. "Then this is justice," he finally said.

Elizabeth looked away and squinted her eyes to see into the woods.

She wanted to be away from here and back to some place she could call "home," but she realized that these Indians had covered the ground she would have to travel to get there. *Justice?* She thought to herself. *Is this how prairie justice works in a place without laws?* She had fleeting thoughts of how law comes to a place. She wondered how long folks would make their own justice.

Everyone remounted and walked their horses away from the death scene.

"They're not going to leave us alone," Smith said. "They believe the whole earth belongs to them."

Milligan and James just looked at each other, not knowing what they might say to Smith. James glanced back at Shag.

"Storm coming, Parker. You better lay in at my place till it passes," Smith said.

Milligan looked at the sky. Clouds were boiling, and there was thunder in the distance. James sniffed the air. Smith was right.

"Thanks, Smith, we'll take you up on that," James said. "Liz-beth, you'll get a woman's visit after-all," he said smiling.

The party arrived at Smith's barn just as the heavens opened up. The rain started, and it continued for three days. Elizabeth was glad for the conversation with Smith's wife, who was glad for the rare company of another woman. Finally, on the morning of the fourth day James, Elizabeth, Milly and Shag resumed their journey to Montgomery.

## Reaching Montgomery — September 6th

On the 6th day of September, James pointed ahead. "There's smoke from our cabin, Elizabeth. We'll be home soon."

Elizabeth looked around to realize that Shag was no longer riding with them.

Soon after, Milly turned off towards the woods. "Until next time," he said as he spurred his horse into a trot.

James and Elizabeth rode on alone a few more miles and finally approached a cabin. Patsey came running to them. Elizabeth started to cry and slid down from her horse. The two women wrapped in each other's arms. Patsey took the reins of Elizabeth's horse, and they walked the rest of the way to the front porch.

Two little barefoot children were there and cried "Daddy" as they reached up to James. He sat on the floor of the little porch and let his children hug him all over.

"You been good for your mama?" he asked them. They both assured him they had been good, and their mother confirmed their claim.

Patsey had been baking bread and slow-roasting meat for days. She had no way of knowing for sure that James would have any of the captives with him when he returned, but his wife always was hopeful when he went away. "I couldn't live with the heaviness if I didn't believe he'd bring somebody back. Every time he leaves, I just focus on getting the place ready to welcome somebody back. You're the first, Elizabeth. You have made us so happy."

At first Elizabeth struggled to contain her emotions. She was angry over her captivity. She was humiliated over the indignities of her exposure

and abuse. She remembered the violence of the raid and flashed back to the vision of the contorted, bloody bodies in the stockade. She didn't know what to say, so she said nothing. This would be her way now, quietly keeping her memories in private. She preferred to spend her time choosing to be happy and playing with Patsey's children.

"What can you tell me about Rachael," Patsey asked. "What happened to the boys? What did they do with Cynthia Ann?"

Elizabeth knew well the horrors Patsey's daughter Rachael and the boys had experienced. But she really didn't know if Rachael was still alive. She doubted the children had been able to survive their abuse. But she couldn't share any of that with Patsey. It would break her heart to know the truth, and there was no way to know their fate. She wanted to leave room for hope of Rachael's return.

"I don't know, Patsey. They separated us." That was the "truth" Elizabeth would live with for the rest of her days. She closed off the past and told herself it didn't happen. She just looked ahead. She only wanted to think about what she could control, which was very, very little. But she could control her words, which might control what people asked of her.

Meanwhile, news had come to James about sightings of white children. Holland Coffee had a well-known trading post out on the Red River. It was due north, two-hundred miles away. The fall season was not yet upon them. Maybe he could make it there and back by winter. James decided he had to try. The very next day he left, as his wife, his children and his sister-in-law waved goodbye.

# Part Six:
# The Final Journey

## Shepperd's General Store — October 5th

It was still dark in Montgomery on a cool night in October. Patsey Parker lit her oil lamp and stepped outside on the front porch. Her sister Elizabeth was shelling pecans by the light of the harvest moon. Her back was bent, and her head was low, deep in concentration on her task.

"Aren't you tired, Sister?"

Elizabeth didn't answer. The front two legs of her chair were off the floor, and she rocked on the back two, loosening the joints of the straight legs. The chair creaked as it went back and forth until it sounded as if the chair would fall apart.

Elizabeth squeezed several fat nuts together in her hand, destroying the brown shells. She tossed the brown meat in a crockery bowl sitting on the floor and threw the shells out into the dirt. She seemed lost in her work.

The moon was high in the sky, and Patsey needed sleep. She dared to ask again. "Elizabeth . . . will you try to sleep tonight?"

Elizabeth lurched and put the chair down on all four legs. She lifted her head and looked straight ahead. "No, Sister. I can't."

In the days and nights she had spent there, Elizabeth tried to sleep, but sleep was always invaded by a face painted with heavy black circles around the eyes. Then giant hands came at her, and she awakened screaming. She wanted to sleep. She would try again, but not tonight. Elizabeth adjusted herself in the chair. Errant pecan shells crunched under her feet, but she didn't seem to notice. She closed her eyes tight, licked her lips and scrunched her shoulders just to loosen them. Then she looked at her sister, and her expression calmed.

"Go to bed, Patsey," she said, so softly her words were barely perceptible. "I'll be fine out here."

Patsey wrapped her arms around the porch post and leaned her head on it. "What can we do, Elizabeth? How can we fix this? You can't go on without sleep."

Elizabeth looked back at Patsey's face. Her sense of herself returned.

Patsey's question brought her back to reality. She reached down and picked up the crockery basin.

"I have to find Benjamin," she said. "We have to get back to Gonzales. I think that's what I need most. Can you please help me with that?" Her voice was as quiet as the night. Her soft words didn't even compete with the crickets. Elizabeth had always been a quiet force, and Patsey knew she never asked for anything. Pleading to find her husband was a powerful thing, coming from Elizabeth. Patsey knew it was probably the only solution to her sister's despairs.

"Yes, you are probably right," Patsey said. The two women held their thoughts and contemplated their plight.

After a time Patsey interrupted the silence. "I have an idea, but it may not get us anywhere. If you are up to it, we can try asking at the Shepperd General Store for help. They post notices there. It's kind of a gathering place for news. Ol' Willy Shepperd knows a lot of people, and he knows what goes on. He's a good man, and if he can, he'll help us."

Elizabeth looked up at her sister. Her eyes opened wide and glistened in the moonlight. Patsey thought she detected the hint of a smile in her sister's lips. She moved closer and put her hands over Elizabeth's grip on the bowl. "We'll get some help, don't you worry. If not from Shepperd's, then from somewhere else."

"But Shepperd's General is a good place to start," Elizabeth said. "Let's go tomorrow, can we?"

"Sure. We'll go in the morning." Patsey stood and held the door open, hoping her sister would come inside.

Elizabeth turned her face to the woods. "Good night," she said.

Patsey closed the door and collapsed on her bed.

The next morning Patsey stepped out onto the porch before the sun was up. Elizabeth was standing at the porch post looking out into the prairie. "How soon can we go?" she said, without turning around.

"We can go now," her sister said. "I told the children to stay in the house till I get back." Elizabeth started walking toward town, and Patsey ran to catch up to her.

Elizabeth looked around at the community of Montgomery. It was on a road leading to Harrisburg, which was sixty miles south. Settled as far back as 1831 and spared the Mexican torch, it was buzzing the way Gonzales had back in '34. "Let's go in here." Patsey took her sister's hand and led her up two steps, into the general store.

"Howdy, Mrs. Parker. What can I get you today?" A hefty man with a round, red face welcomed them. He was short, and his legs bowed out at the knees. Thick, sand-colored hair encircled his face, and he spoke through a bush of whiskers.

"Willy, it's good to see you," Patsey said. "We're not really in need of supplies today, but we need some information."

Elizabeth had been away from white settlements so long, she stopped listening and looked around her. She was taking it all in: the road, the store, the inventory. Boxes, crates and barrels were stacked in rows. Behind a long counter she noticed iron skillets, fire pokers, mule collars and wagon parts. In the corner stood a new pair of leather boots marked "2 dollars." Everything was coated with dust, and Elizabeth knew that nothing here had been displaced the way Gonzales had been. She was lost in her memories when Patsey tugged on her arm.

"Did you hear that, Elizabeth? Willy knows a man that can help us."

"Yes'm. You just wait here, and I'll go fetch him." Willy went out the door.

Patsey walked around the store, and Elizabeth leaned on a barrel marked "pickles."

## Joe Bogs — October 6th

"Let's go sit on the porch and wait," Patsey said. Elizabeth followed her sister and began to ask about Willy.

"What did he tell you? Where is he going?"

After the sisters settled on chairs out front of the store, Patsey explained, "I told him that you need to go find your husband in Harrisburg. There is a ranging group here, and they don't have work just now," she said as she craned her neck to see down the only street running through the town. "It's not like we don't have trouble." She flicked at a bothersome fly as she spoke. "No, there's plenty of reports of trouble. But there's no money to pay the Rangers, so they don't go out."

Patsey fanned herself with her flat hand. "James tried to get help." Patsey looked at her sister and thought about how she could explain her husband's efforts to search for Elizabeth and the others. "Well, it's just been confusing, with the change in government and all. James is still trying to get help from the Rangers to look for Rachael and the children. But there is no money in the government, and they just can't go."

Patsey stood up and pointed up the street. "Oh, look," she said. She saw Willy Shepperd and another man coming their way. "Here they come back now." The ladies waited as the men's boots crunched the stones with each step. When he reached them, Willy introduced his companion.

"Mrs. Parker, this here is Joe Bogs. He makes unofficial runs to Harrisburg right often these days," Willy said.

Patsey nodded and Mr. Bogs nodded back.

"Come on in here and tell me what you need, ma'am." Mr. Bogs removed his leather hat with a small, muscular hand. He was clean-shaven. His face was tan and taut. Elizabeth sat quietly and left the conversation to her sister.

"I'll go explain it to him, Sister. You stay here." Patsey followed Willy into the general store, and Mr. Bogs followed.

Elizabeth stayed in her chair on the porch in front of the general store, feeling very uneasy. She tried to be as small and discreet as possible. As men walked along the street, she hoped no one knew who she was. James and Patsey had lived here a while, and James had talked in town openly and often about his efforts to rescue his family members. She also thought about the Ranger and what he might want in payment for his work. A lot of questions passed through her head, but no answers came.

What seemed to Elizabeth like a long wait finally came to an end. Patsey came out of the general store looking as joyful as a woman could look in those dreadful days. "He'll take you now, Sister, right now!" she announced. She came to her sister's chair and knelt at her side. She took her sister's hands and looked in Elizabeth's eyes. In a quieter voice she repeated, "He can take you to Harrisburg today, if you really want to go."

Elizabeth liked to ponder things in life, but today she knew she would have to decide quickly. "I'll go," she said quietly. "Yes, I'll go on with him now, if that's what we need to do."

Mr. Bogs stepped out of the doorway just as Elizabeth made her decision.

"She'll go with you, sir," Patsey told him.

He pointed to Elizabeth with his hat rolled up in his hand. "You stay right there, and I'll be right back," he said. The ladies watched as Mr. Bogs went toward a small shed down the street.

Patsey continued to explain, "The Rangers don't have work just now, Elizabeth. Our luck, Mr. Bogs says he's been yearning for some work, and this was just the thing. He says he can get you to Harrisburg in three days."

Elizabeth nodded and looked down.

"You'll have to ride a horse; can you do that?"

Elizabeth nodded and looked up at her sister. Her heart was pounding in her throat, realizing what might lay ahead of her in just a few days. How could she explain it all? "Patsey, does Mr. Bogs know about me?"

"Yes, Sister, but he knows a lot of things." Patsey took her green crocheted shawl and wrapped her sister's shoulders. "Mr. Bogs has been bringing captives back for years, Elizabeth. He's not going to judge you or tell anybody about your past. His job is just to get you to Harrisburg, and then he'll help find Benjamin. Think of it, Elizabeth! We couldn't have found a better man for the job." Elizabeth pulled the shawl tighter and wrapped the tail of it around her fingers.

"Bogs knows Harrisburg. He spent a lot of time there. I told him about the steamboats. He feels quite sure he can find Benjamin. He said he's certain he can do it with no trouble." Patsey tried to smooth Elizabeth's hair, and she tucked some loose strands behind her ear.

Elizabeth's thoughts raced to what she would say to her husband. Did he know of her capture? If not, how would she tell him? Would he want her back? Then her thoughts returned to the immediate task at hand, the "hiring" of Mr. Bogs.

"Oh, Patsy, how can I pay Mr. Bogs for his work? Days and days we'll be on the road, and then the bother we'll find in Harrisburg. He'll have to search the town for Benjamin. How can he do all that? I need to pay him."

Patsey took her sister's hands. "Do you remember the day of the raid, Elizabeth? Before the Indians came in, you gave me and Mama coins. Mine were big yellow coins. I've been saving them. I've given one to Mr. Bogs. So in reality . . . you already paid him."

Elizabeth tilted her head and remembered before the screaming started on that day many months ago. Then, suddenly it did come back to her. She gasped and her eyes went wide. "Oh, Patsey! After all this time, you still had the coins I gave you? What a wonderful thing . . . I can't believe it." Elizabeth's mind raced over the simple life she had seen at Patsey's place. She remembered the kindnesses Patsey had shown her. She knew the coins could have been used for her sister's comforts in many ways.

"That's the kindest, most wonderful thing anyone has ever done for me, Patsey," she said.

"But it came from you, Elizabeth." The two sisters looked at each other in a new way that day. They both knew this could be the last time they saw each other for maybe a long, long time, maybe forever. The promise of earthly life was often broken, and they both knew it. There was nothing more they needed to say, so they shared a long, last hug.

## Harrisburg Again — October 10th

What a difference the months had made. Elizabeth expected to see the dilapidated, abject Harrisburg she knew the day Benjamin buried Sydnie and Charlotte Mexia asked to share a bench. But it looked like a different place.

The Harrisburg Elizabeth saw from her horse as she rode into town with Joe Bogs, that Harrisburg was a boomtown. The temporary camps of the enthusiastic population began a mile farther out. Partially burned buildings were now repaired, and reconstruction was buzzing. The air was thick with the assaulting noise of hammers and saws. The business of rebuilding dominated everything else.

Elizabeth felt invigorated by the energy of the town. There was a mysterious and eerie sense of "belonging," even though the city had changed. Maybe because she knew Sydnie was near and she expected to find Benjamin. The vitality around her generated a sense of hope, and she produced a smile. Mr. Bogs noticed it and smiled back at her.

"Turn this way," he said as he nodded to his right and pulled the reins that way. He seemed totally unconfused by the chaos of the city. He rode his horse up one trail and down another, turning with intention either left or right, often going straight several blocks. Elizabeth followed slightly behind him as the new Harrisburg revealed itself.

After what Elizabeth thought had been a very circuitous route, he stopped in front of a long, narrow wooden building. The walls were patched with new wood, and the windows and entrance doorway were just framed openings in the front wall. A sign was over the building. The hastily painted words "Angel's Place" stoked her curiosity.

Mr. Bogs cleared his throat, leaned forward, and put both hands on his saddle horn, "Mrs. Kellogg, I'm going to need to find the headquarters for the work crews at the docks," he explained. "They'll have some kind of head place where the boss men have records of everybody working in town. I'll go find it, but you need to wait here till I get back."

Elizabeth swallowed hard and looked at the building in front of her. "Angel's Place?" she asked. It sounded like a brothel. Her imagination was racing, but surely the Ranger would not be insulting her by leaving her in such a place. "You mean for me to wait in here for you?" She looked at him with her eyebrows raised.

Joe Bogs seemed sober, and without a shred of mockery he said, "Yes, ma'am. You go in there and ask for Angel. She'll take good care of you till I get back."

Elizabeth knew she had no options. This was her lot now, to be at the mercy of those she asked for help. If this was a white man's ridicule because of her captivity she would deal with it at the right time. So far, no one had mistreated her, so she would not make assumptions. If this was a questionable place where people expected women to do questionable things, she would protest inside. She wanted Bogs to go find Benjamin, and so she would do as he said.

She squinted her eyes and slid down from her horse.

"I'll take his reins," Bogs said, and she strained her arms to hand him the long leather straps. She felt vulnerable, wondering if anyone was watching her prepare to enter what she anticipated was the kind of place she had never been. She looked around. No one seemed to notice her. She looked at Bogs, who looked at her with the same respect he had always shown her.

"Angel?" she asked. She wrapped herself in her sister's green shawl.

"Yes, ask for Angel," Joe Bogs said as he nudged his horse and pulled on the reins in his hands. He walked two horses up the street and left Elizabeth standing on the street in front of "Angel's Place."

## Angel's Place — October 10th

Elizabeth walked up the steps and went through the unfinished doorway to "Angel's Place."

"Howdy, honey," a voice said. Inside the building sat a short, squatty woman. "What can I do for you?" she asked Elizabeth.

"Oh, hello," Elizabeth began. It was dim inside, and she waited for her eyes to adjust. She put up her pointing finger in her characteristic way to indicate that she was going to say something.

"Mr. Joe Bogs brought me here, ma'am," she said as the woman's face came into focus. "He told me to ask for someone named Angel."

"That's Joe Bogs, my favorite nephew!" the woman shouted, coming closer to Elizabeth. She smiled, revealing a mouth with several teeth missing. "I ain't seen that boy in a coon's age! Where is he?" she said, standing in the doorless entrance, looking right and left. Elizabeth noticed as the woman reached across the doorway that one of her hands had most of the fingers missing.

"I don't know, ma'am. He just told me to wait here till he gets back."

"Well, honey, you just come over here, and let's get you a place to light," the woman said. "I'm his Antie-Angel. Joe knew I'd love to have some company."

The old woman was very round and crooked in her back. She walked with a sway and made a swooshing noise as she went.

"Set down right here and tell me, what brings you to town?" She poured herself a glass of something golden, squatted on a wooden crate, crossed her arms over the top of a barrel and waited for Elizabeth to explain herself.

Elizabeth was again stumped as to exactly how to clarify her situation. "Well, ma'am, Mr. Bogs is going to get my husband. He's working here . . . somewhere, in town." She propped herself across from the barrel against the wall. The two women looked at each other silently sorting out what brought them together. In her mind Angel was filling in the missing information about her guest.

"Then I suppose you'll be wantin' a place over the night," Angel said as she took a drink.

"Yes, ma'am. I suppose that's what I'll be needing," Elizabeth agreed.

"Well, I'm just delighted to have you stay here with me for as short or as long as you need," she said. "You just follow me, and we'll get you a cozy place back out here."

She led Elizabeth out the back door where three make-shift camps were set out.

Angel had collected salvage from Harrisburg and made good use of it all. Lengths of post oak framed three little camping spaces. Sections of clapboard were laid over the frame, making an efficient ceiling. A run of pine planks made a walkway against the dirt floor. The remains of bedframes were laced with a variety of heavy rope to serve as a hammock. A salvaged chair sat in each little camp, waiting for someone to sit there, never mind the broken backs or mended legs.

"Pick your spot," Angel said to Elizabeth.

Elizabeth chose the camp nearest the main building and stepped into the space. Large nails jutted out from timbers across the back of the shelter, ready to hang clothing. A large trunk sat at the end of the bed. Just beyond the camps was a privy, emitting the odor of urine.

Elizabeth contemplated the shelters. She recalled the nights she was strung up to the tree limb. She hunched her shoulders to remind herself what she had survived. She closed her eyes and was thankful for this safe little space.

Angel pulled a key out of her apron pocket and unlatched the lid to the trunk. She reached inside and pulled out a bundle of canvas and sections of rope. She had devised a way to wrap the canvas around the corner posts of the space when it was occupied, making a sort of tent enclosure.

"You come help me and we'll put up some walls," Angel said. "I only put this up when I need it. I can't leave it, or it'll disappear!!" she laughed. "Everybody's need'n somethin'. Anythin' you got, somebody's need'n."

Elizabeth looked around toward the privy and wrinkled her nose.

"Just like that," Angel said, gesturing toward the tiny enclosure. "Folks come use my outhouse," she said. "But that's alright. We gotta share what we got now, don't you think so?"

They untied the bundle and worked together to wrap the canvas around the corner framing boards as much as possible. The edges of the canvas were fixed with holes cut just-so as to allow the fabric to be tied to the corner posts and make a fabric wall.

Elizabeth tried her best to raise her arms to hold the canvas to the corner posts. Pain stabbed into her shoulders, and she winced.

Angel made no mention of Elizabeth's limitation but suggested a way out of the predicament. "Let me do the high part," Angel said as she took the corner and raised it high. "You just hold it onto the pole about waist-high so it don't pull loose."

"This works just fine," Angel said as she tied off the canvas edges. Elizabeth was impressed with Angel's agility with her partial hand.

"I don't get much company, but when they do stay, folks seem fairly comfortable in here. You'll see, honey. You'll get some sleep, and you'll be just fine in here till Joe-Boy gets back."

Angel was hungry for a woman's company, and Elizabeth was thankful to be with her. "You come back in with me now, and let's drink some coffee," Angel said.

Elizabeth didn't have any possessions except for the green crocheted shawl her sister had wrapped around her shoulders at the general store back in Montgomery. She left the shawl in the trunk and closed the lid. Angel winked at Elizabeth and nodded her head, "Good thinking," she said. Angel pulled a long, heavy key out of her apron pocket and handed it to her new tenant. "Give this a turn in the lock, and we'll be sure your shawl is safe."

Elizabeth took the key and locked the huge trunk. Her memories flashed back to the day of the raid, when Grannie climbed into their family trunk to find the coins. The screaming began to build up in her head. She shut her eyes and shook her head.

"You okay, honey?" Angel asked.

Elizabeth smiled and handed Angel the key. "It's nothing, ma'am. Some coffee would be really good, though."

Angel slipped the key into her pocket. She squinted her eyes, linked her hands behind her back and swooshed toward the back door of her building.

The two women went inside Angel's Place. Angel set a kettle on the woodstove where a tiny glow came from the coals. She rolled a tree stump out from the corner. "Sit down here and tell me 'bout yourself, honey."

"Not much to tell, ma'am," Elizabeth said as she propped herself on the stump.

Angel nodded. Without any words she opened the little door of the stove. She took a worn, slender stick, stirred the hot coals, and closed the door. She put the burned tip of the stick into a hole on top of the stove, fussed with the kettle and found two tin cups. She wiped out the cups with her apron and sat them on a rough-cut strip of wood she used for a table. Neither of them spoke for a spell. Then Angel broke the silence.

"That Ol' Bogs, I tell you what," she said as she cocked her head to one side. "That boy, he's a good one. You wouldn't know it, but he's been my Joe-Boy for thirty years. My little brother's boy, he is. Come down from Memphis to help out 'round here," she made a little smacking sound with the corner of her mouth and winked her eye at Elizabeth.

She shivered a bit and propped her elbows on the tabletop. "He come to help with the buildin' and the settlin'." She looked out the window opening. "Turned out there's a lot more than that to do," she said with a voice that trialed off a bit, and then she stared silently down the street for a time.

After what looked like some reflection on her part, the old woman jerked herself back to the present. She reached under the stove and pulled out a corncob pipe. "Joe-Boy been helping with the Indian troubles, you know," she said over her shoulder.

She pulled the burning stick out of the hole in the top of the stove and took a seat to wait for the kettle to heat.

She held the burning stick between the thumb and pointer finger of her crippled hand and held the pipe in her left hand. She lit the thing and took several long draws.

"You prob'ly don't know nothin' 'bout Indian troubles... a sweet thing like you." She carefully replaced the stick on the stove top, looked at Elizabeth, pursed her lips together and nodded. There was another long quiet spell.

Angel leaned back against the wall. She crossed her right arm against her chest and held the pipe in the left. Elizabeth wondered how her hand was taken.

Angel looked at the kettle and then out the window again, toward the road out front. "Lots of heartache out there," she said. "The only hope we have is what we make for ourselves." She took another long draw on her pipe. "Joe-Boy feeds his soul with rescuin' folks." She turned back around to Elizabeth.

"They killed his wife in a most terrible way," she said. "Took my hand that day." She held up the two-fingered slice of a hand, turned it and looked it over. "Yep, he knows." She said. "But best if you don't know nothin' 'bout that, honey. I'm just sayin' whatever it is you're needin' from my nephew, he's glad to do it."

Elizabeth closed her eyes, wishing this trial was over. She longed for days when the stories people told were happy ones. She believed there would be more happy stories, but she also knew they would take a while.

Meanwhile, Elizabeth thought Angel might be just who her name implied, a sacred spirit sent to earth, disguised as a worn-out woman who knew instinctively about secret horrors that should stay secret. Elizabeth diverted her eyes. In the dim light of the ramshackle structure Angel called home, Elizabeth searched for clues about her hostess.

The kettle began to make a popping sound. Angel put her pipe deep into a large dried gourd sitting in the frame of the window opening. She made her way to the stove. She pulled a crumpled bandana from a pile of toweling, wrapped it around the stumpy hand and removed the pot from the hot stove top. She poured what appeared to be muddy water into the two tins and passed one to Elizabeth.

Elizabeth blew over the liquid, pretending she was planning on drinking it.

Angel put the kettle back onto the stove. She slipped her good hand into the handle of her cup and took a little slurp. She crossed her right arm over her chest and began to reminisce about her life.

"I'm eighty-eight years old last month, young lady," she winked and nodded at Elizabeth. The old woman's eyes drifted off into the space of the building. "I faced down bears and Injuns in my time." She held onto that memory for a moment as she sipped again from the cup. "That Mexican army came through our place and ran over my man and my son." The twinkle in her eye and the peace of her face slowly transformed into a somber expression. Her eyes hazed over as the memories closed in. She looked down at the floor and shook her head. Her voice drifted off unintelligibly. Then she turned her face to Elizabeth. "I already faced the devil himself, honey. Whatever you're facing—whatever Joe-Boy is helping you with—you can take it."

Elizabeth didn't know how to respond. To her good fortune, a man came in through the door opening and asked for directions to somebody's farm. The distraction was well placed, and it gave Elizabeth a chance to gather her wits. Angel went outside to point her directions. Elizabeth took advantage of the opportunity to pour the muddy liquid back into the kettle. Then she sat back down on her stool until Angel returned.

"I'd really like to sleep now, ma'am," Elizabeth told her hostess. "I think my trials are catching up with me."

"I'll go with you to open the trunk, and you can settle in for the evening," Angel said. "Let's get you some blankets."

Elizabeth and Angel went out the back of the old woman's shelter, picking up three nicely folded blankets along the way.

## Finding Benjamin — October 11th

"Good mornin', ma'am." Joe Bogs' steady voice came from the corner table where he sat drinking Angel's thick coffee as Elizabeth came in the back door. He'd been there a while. His head was bare of his hat. He stood up and pulled out a chair for Elizabeth, and she noticed his feet were also bare of his boots.

With a swoosh of her body in the tight space, Angel delivered a sizzling skillet onto the center of the table. Chunks of sausage, slabs of bread and some apple slices were all slathered with something that glistened like butter. They were perfectly grilled, with crispy edges. With her two-fingered-hand she slipped another tin of coffee in front of Elizabeth.

Elizabeth nodded her gratitude as she held the tin cup in her hands. "Did you find my Benjamin?" she asked Mr. Bogs.

"How'd you sleep, ma'am?" he asked.

Elizabeth was put off by his evasiveness, but buying into his tactic, she politely answered his question with a convenient lie.

"I slept fine, Mr. Bogs." She waited while he sipped his coffee. He leaned to his side and pulled out a folding knife from his pocket. He opened the knife blade and stabbed a bit of sausage. Angel slipped a two-pronged fork on the table near Elizabeth. Without realizing it, Elizabeth took in a breath and held it, waiting for the news Bogs might have.

Joe Bogs wrapped his thumb in his handkerchief and gently shoved the sizzling skillet closer to Elizabeth as he chewed.

After what seemed to Elizabeth like much too long, Mr. Bogs swallowed and wiped his mouth on his handkerchief. He pushed back a bit from the table and crossed one long leg over the other. "Yes, I found your husband," he said with a tone of indifference. His face was emotionless, his eyes looking steely at his client.

Elizabeth's breath staggered as she let out her breath. She let the words replay in her head. *The man said, "yes." Benjamin is somewhere near. Very near. But not here. Bogs had not brought him back to her.*

"Why didn't he come with you?" Elizabeth asked. "Can I go to him? Is he working? Did you tell him I'm here?" She had so many questions she didn't know which one should be answered first. Her thoughts came tumbling out.

Privately she had more questions that she dared not ask. She wanted to know if Benjamin knew of her captivity; did he know, and was that why he didn't come to her? Was she an embarrassment of the family now? Would he refuse to see her after she had disgraced him? But Elizabeth had not even discussed these things with Angel and certainly not Mr. Bogs. Those things she wouldn't be discussing now.

"He's sick, Mrs. Kellogg."

Elizabeth jerked her head at the sudden information. "Sick? What kind of sick?" she asked.

"I don't know, ma'am. I found him through his boss-man over at the docks. I didn't talk to him. He's been in the infirmary about a week now."

Mr. Bogs stabbed an apple slice and pressed it against a chunk of the crusty bread, making the apple squash out like butter. He reached for the bread and held it. "I didn't see him, they just told me he was there. I asked the foreman to let him know about you being here." He took a bite of the bread.

"Can I go see him? Can you take me to him?"

Mr. Bogs thought for a minute. "Mrs. Kellogg, you'd be better off not going in there."

"But I have to. I have to see him," Elizabeth leaned in close to Mr. Bogs, trying to suppress her anxiety, yet voicing her insistence. "That's why I came, Mr. Bogs. It's my only purpose now. You have to take me to him."

"Ma'am, the docks are a dangerous place now. A lot of disease over there," he tried to explain.

It was another demonstrative and animated conversation. She forgot herself for a moment and in a rare display, much like she had appealed to James in Nacogdoches, she uncharacteristically revealed her desperation.

She doubled her fist and almost growled. "Mr. Bogs. I have to see him," she said.

Then she caught herself and reeled her emotions back in.

"Yes, I understand," Bogs said. "Your husband can't work just now. Have you thought about where you'll stay? Do you want to go back to Montgomery to your sister?"

"No, not there," Elizabeth said. "I want to get back to Gonzales. That's our home. We have family there."

Mr. Bogs' confidence didn't increase. The look on his face offered no optimism. "That's a long trip," he said.

"I've already come a long way, Mr. Bogs," Elizabeth said grimly. She privately remembered the beatings she had taken. She hunched her damaged shoulders and remembered her struggle to get up on the painted pony she rode into Nacogdoches and the trip to Montgomery. "This is not my first stay in Harrisburg, sir."

Bogs looked at Elizabeth and realized he had hit a tender cord. He couldn't know that today she stood here where her journey started just three months before, having come full circle, and gone the long way around. He didn't know about her losses at the Alamo and about Sydnie, and she wasn't going to tell him.

After a few minutes of thought she added, "I need to ask Benjamin what he wants to do. If you can get me to him, I can ask him. Then we will know what to do."

"Yes, ma'am," he continued. "I have some ideas." He motioned to Angel to come back to their table.

Angel flipped a towel over her left shoulder and swayed over to the place where Joe Bogs sat with Elizabeth.

"Angel, this woman needs more help," Bogs started his appeal. "Can I bring her husband here for a few days?"

Angel looked at Elizabeth. She reared back and brought her two hands together in front of her. "I think we can do whatever you think best, Joe-Boy."

"I don't know how long they'll need to stay. The man's in bad shape, but if he can make it here, at least we'll have that much done."

Elizabeth thought about how a man could be in bad shape. She remembered seeing Elder John's scalp laced to a pair of Indian boots. Benjamin couldn't be in any worse shape than that.

"You bring him here, and we'll see how that goes," Angel said. "They can stay out in that first camp as long as they need to."

Elizabeth was sizing up her obligations, weighing what she needed against what she had in the way of resources. "I don't know how I can ever repay you," she said to Angel and Mr. Bogs.

"If folks only got what they can repay, nobody would get nothin' around here," Angel said with a bit of a laugh. "If we don't help each other, this Texas will never be a fittin' place. One day you may be back here to help me, honey. Who knows how things will work out. For now, you need a camp; I happen to have a camp. You let Joe-Boy bring your husband in, and we'll go from there."

"Ma'am, your sister paid me. That'll be enough to take care of whatever you need for now. Don't worry about the cost. Just wait here and I'll go see if I can bring Benjamin back." Mr. Bogs tilted his head back and settled his broad-brimmed hat back into place. He reached to his side and pulled on his boots.

Elizabeth sat back and nodded. Again, she had limited options, but this option was golden.

When Joe Bogs left Angel's Place he went to the livery where he stabled his horse in trade for a mule and a wagon. Then he went back to the docks to search among the sick for Benjamin Kellogg.

## Last Night in Harrisburg — October 11th

The day passed quickly, and Joe Bogs walked the mule up the road, bringing the little cart to a slow stop in front of Angel's Place. Elizabeth walked out to the boardwalk and looked toward the shallow-sided wagon. Inside she saw a long bundle wrapped in a gray wool blanket.

As she approached the wagon, she heard a low moan. She held her hands together at her chin and listened.

"He's delirious, ma'am," Mr. Bogs explained.

Elizabeth stepped back. She had wondered what their reunion would be, but she hadn't expected delirium.

"Let's pull this rig around to the back, and I'll help you get him out."

Angel and Elizabeth met the wagon behind Angel's Place, and together the three of them carried Benjamin, wrapped in the blanket, and laid him on the bedding Elizabeth had prepared for him.

Benjamin's eyes stayed closed. He moaned and groaned and paid them no mind.

"He never knew I was there," Bogs said. "The people at the infirmary said he took a turn for the worse last night. I tried to tell him I was bringing him to see you, but I don't know if he heard me."

With her attention on her husband Elizabeth thanked Mr. Bogs. "You did all you can, and I thank you," she said as she pulled the gray wool away from Benjamin's face.

Bogs and Angel stood aside. Angel looked at Bogs and shook her head ever-so-slightly. "I'll get you some water and some towels," Angel said as she left the Kellogg's camp.

Benjamin Kellogg was shaking. They gray wool blanket was damp with his sweat. He curled his fingers around the edge of the blanket and gripped it tightly.

Angel came back with a basin of shallow water and some toweling. "Wipe his face. Maybe that will make him feel better."

Elizabeth was kneeling by her husband. She tried to hold his hand, but he fretted and pitched and pulled away. He moaned and rolled his head from side to side. His face, typically tan and full of color from his hours in the sun, was white as a cloud and splotched with gray. His cheeks caved in under the peaks of his bones, and there were deep blue crevices around his eye sockets.

Elizabeth dipped a towel into the water and wiped his face. As the damp cloth went across his lips, his tongue came out to chase the moisture. Elizabeth squeezed the cloth, and a trickle of water made its way along Benjamin's mouth and between his lips. He licked at the dribble and opened his eyes.

Upon seeing his wife Benjamin's agitation calmed. His eyes searched her face as if he was remembering her. In the quietness of the moment he captured her gaze and held it for a long, long time.

"Benjamin," she said.

He blinked and nodded his head ever so little.

"Benjamin, I've come to take you home."

Calm overcame him. The shivering stopped. He looked at Joe Bogs kneeling by the bed, and then he looked back at his wife.

Elizabeth put her hand over Benjamin's hand as he closed his eyes. His face relaxed, and he fell asleep. Angel took two blankets from the trunk and laid them over Benjamin, hoping he could stay warm now.

"I'll be back to check on you later," Angel said. Bogs stood up and he walked out of the camp with his aunt.

As dusk fell Angel came to check on the couple. She brought Elizabeth a hefty chunk of hot bread and more thick, hot coffee. Elizabeth nibbled at her treats throughout the sleepless night. Angel came in twice more. Benjamin never moved.

Early the next morning Elizabeth heard the crunch of boots in the rocks outside her camp. Mr. Joe Bogs had come to check on his client-friends. "Elizabeth, you go take a break. I'll stay out here till you get back."

Without much expression a very weary and exhausted Elizabeth stood up. She looked down at the bundle lying under all the blankets. Benjamin's fingers were still tightly clutching the edge of the gray wool, and he appeared to be smiling peacefully. She looked at him a long time, and then she stepped outside the camp.

When he knew she was away, Joe Bogs knelt by Benjamin's bed. He pulled at the edge of the blanket and lifted the man's hand. The fingers were locked tight, and Bogs forced them open. Finally, he was able to feel for a pulse in the wrist. Nothing.

In the process of opening Ben's hand, a five-dollar gold piece fell onto the dirt floor below the bed.

Bogs put the coin into his shirt pocket and pulled out a cigarette paper. A feather was wrapped in the paper. It was a tiny bit of bird-lace, with only threads of down that would sway from even the lightest breath. He placed the feather in front of Benjamin's nose. Nothing moved. He placed the feather on the man's upper lip. While he waited for the feather to move his fingers rubbed the coin in his shirt pocket. After several minutes there was still no movement, because there was no breath coming in or coming out. He was convinced. There was no life left in Benjamin Kellogg.

Joe Bogs stood outside the opening of the Kellogg camp as Elizabeth came back. He reached out and put a hand on each of her shoulders. Elizabeth studied his face while he considered his words. "I'm sorry, ma'am. You can't help him anymore."

Elizabeth didn't react. She wasn't surprised. With a conciliatory tone she looked away. "I know," she said.

"He's gone now," Bogs explained.

"I know," she repeated.

"Let's go in and talk to Angel," Joe said quietly. Elizabeth turned to go.

"Wait just a minute," Joe said. He reached into his pocket and took out the gold coin. "He had this in his hand," he said. "It almost felt like he didn't want to give it up, but I know he'd want you to have it."

As Elizabeth took the coin, she remembered the anguish in Benjamin's face the night she gave it to him. He said it would be his inspiration, and now it would be hers.

"Thank you, Mr. Bogs. Now I can go home and start over," she said.

Elizabeth and Mr. Bogs walked through the back door of Angel's Place. Angel was standing over a large basin of dishes, drying them and setting them in a crate. She flipped the towel over her shoulder and brought her two hands together at her chin. She didn't say anything. She looked first at Elizabeth and then at her nephew.

"Angel, I'm gonna go get the authorities," Joe explained. He tightened his lips and nodded his head discreetly toward Elizabeth, urging his aunt to attend to her.

"Oh, Elizabeth. Come over here, honey," she said. Angel reached out and ushered her guest to one of the log stools. Elizabeth walked stiffly to where she was led, and sat quietly, staring into space.

Angel sat near Elizabeth, and they were both quiet.

After a long while Elizabeth's eyes focused on Angel's face. "Death," she said. "It's all around us. When will it leave us alone?"

Angel took a long, deep breath. She wrapped her arms around Elizabeth, and they rocked together.

# Part Seven:
# The Journeys Are Over

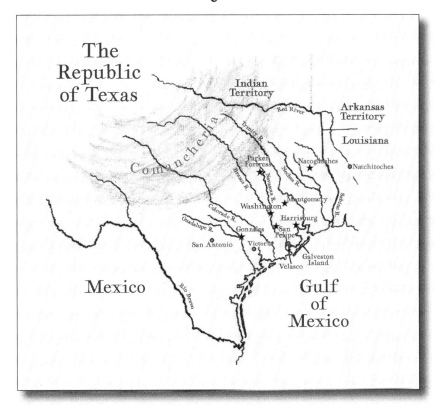

# Gonzales Again — January 1838

On a brisk day in January of 1838, Elizabeth awakened just before the morning sun. In the pre-dawn she went out to the front porch of her cabin wrapped in a green crocheted shawl. She settled into a rocking chair, which began the familiar screech of its joints as she rocked.

The sun rose in the northeast, and she remembered again those who laid in the ground many miles away in that direction, just as she did every morning. Joe Bogs had taken Benjamin and laid him with Sydnie and her dead companions back there near the bayou in Harrisburg. Elizabeth had washed her hands of the horrors she had known in those far-away places. She came back to Gonzales to remember only the good times, and here she would make more of those.

Just as she knew it would happen, the silhouette of a child began to form on the horizon. She thought momentarily about little James Pratt, Cynthia Ann and her brother John Richard. She had gotten word that Rachael was back home, and that pleased her greatly.

As the silhouette became a real child, the taller form of a woman came into focus. They were only figures in the bright morning light, but there was no doubt in Elizabeth's mind who they were.

Two-year-old John Benjamin Kellogg brought his grandmother Rebecca Davis every morning to see his grandmother Elizabeth. It was a time just for the three of them.

Rebecca carried a basket of peaches and fresh bread to the porch while Elizabeth hugged her little grandson. The resilient folks of Gonzales had done amazing things since their return from the Sabine. George Davis had prepared a cluster of tiny cabins with a family water well and a privy out back, right there on St. Louis Street where Sydnie had lived in the early days. Just two years ago when Elizabeth stepped off the coach, George and Rebecca greeted her. "We've been expecting you," they said. "And we have everything ready for you to stay."

And so, she would stay. She would stay for the rest of her life. And for all her days she would awaken to the joy of her grandson's visit. She would close her mind to the losses of her past and count her blessings.

She remembered Charlotte Mexia's kindness and the smile on her mother's face when she arrived at the Parker family fortress. She would be forever grateful to James Parker for her rescue and to Sam Houston for his ransom money. Like so many of the women of the pioneer days in Texas, Elizabeth Kellogg lived with anonymity and a dauntless spirit in her soul.

# Afterword

These are the real people whose documented life events helped me put together this story. Information about their lives can be located in the sources listed in this book.

### Kellogg Family Members

John Benjamin Kellogg I – died in Harrisburg in October 1836.
Elizabeth Duty Kellogg* – captured by Comanches in May 1836; died in Gonzales in 1838.
Sidney Kellogg – gave birth to J.B. Kellogg III in March 1836; died shortly after the Runaway Scrape.
John B. Kellogg II – died at the Alamo on March 6, 1836.
John B. Kellogg III – born March 12, 1836 during the Runaway Scrape; died in 1882 and is buried in Pilgrim Cemetery near Gonzales.

### Parker Family Members

Elder John Parker          Benjamin Parker
Grannie Duty Parker        James Parker
Rachael Duty Plummer*      Silas Parker
James Pratt Plummer*       Patsey Duty Parker
John Richard Parker*       Lucy Duty Parker
Cynthia Ann Parker*

### Mexia Family Members

Charlotte Mexia            Anthony Mexia
Adolpho Mexia              Aldelaida Matilda Mexia
Enrique Guillermo Antonio Mexia

### Other Real People Who Appear in the Story

General Sam Houston, who gave the money for Elizaeth's ransom
Mr. W. Shepperd at the Montgomery General Store
George and Rebecca Davis, grandparents of John B. Kellogg III
The Kiowa who traded Elizabeth to the Delaware
The Delaware who sold Elizabeth to James Parker
The Comanche who was found in East Texas wearing the scalp of Benjamin Parker
The farmer named Smith on whose property the Comanche was found

*Captured during the raid at the Parker Fortress on May 19, 1836.

## Family tree from Sydnie (Sidney) Gaston to the author

John Benjamin Kellogg II + Sydnie Gaston = John Benjamin Kellogg III
|
John Benjamin Kellogg III + Alcinda Elizabeth Breeden = W. Crockett Kellogg
|
W. Crockett Kellogg + Lou Emma Whitehead = Florence Kellogg
|
Florence Kellogg + Oscar Vickers = Brandon Vickers
|
Brandon Vickers + Urvine Rodgers = Betsy Vickers Wagner

# Memo to Readers

It was suggested that I provide some discussion questions for book clubs. I will offer some ideas for discussion below:

- Can you relate to the desire Elizabeth might have had to detach herself from her past?

- How can we account for the differences in levels of aggression among the Indigenous people presented in this story?

- In what ways do you see individuals influencing their own fate by the choices they made? In which situations was their fate totally beyond their influence? How does this relate to life in Texas today?

- What, if any, parts of the story evoked emotion for you? (Anger, sorrow, hope, humor, etc.)

- Considering the range of experiences presented in this story, how different was life in early Texas as compared to life in Texas today? (Violence, homelessness, opportunities for business, family ties, travel).

- Which communities in the story have you visited? Are there some you haven't visited that you would like to visit because of their place in history?

# Sources

## Books

*Return: The Parker Story*, Jack K. Sheldon

*The Indians of Texas*, W.W. Newcomb

*Ride the Wind*, Lucia St. Clair Robson

*Where the Broken Heart Still Beats: The Story of Cynthia Ann Parker*, Carolyn Meyer

*Recollections of Early Texas: Memoirs of John Holland Jenkins*, John Holmes Jenkins

*The Evolution of a State or Recollections of Old Texas Days*, Noah Smithwick

*Texas Tears and Texas Sunshine*, Jo Ella Powell Exley

*Frontier Blood: The Saga of the Parker Family*, Jo Ella Powell Exley

*Texas Baptists: A Sesquicentennial History*, Leon McBeth


## Miscellaneous Sources

*The Early History of Montgomery, Texas*, Kameron K. Searle, J.D.

*Most Desperate People: The Genesis of Texas Exceptionalism*, Michael G. Kelley (dissertation, Georgia State University)

*Gail Borden, Texas Pioneer, Quirky Visionary*, Gary Hoover, Archbridge Institute

*Memoirs of George W. Davis*, family papers

"General Jose Antonio Mexia," Alan Hutchinson, *Southwestern Quarterly*, October 1978

# Internet Sources

FindaGrave page for Elder John Parker,
https:www.findagrave.com/memorial/7433560

Wagon Train from Illinois to Texas, incomplete list
of inhabitants of the thirty-one family wagon train
organized by Reverand Daniel Parker
http://jordan-family.org/texas/

John Benjamin Kellogg's WikiTree page,
http://www.wikitree.com/wiki/kellogg-881

Elder John Parker Wikipedia page,
https://en.wikipedia.org/wiki/John_Parker_(pioneer)

Fort Parker Massacre Wikipedia page,
https://en.wikipedia.org/wiki/Fort_Parker_massacre

The Bible of Daniel Parker,
https://parkerheritage.ning.com/photo/the-bible-of-daniel-parker

Map of 1836 military campaign showing the movements
of the Mexican and Texian armies, http://latinamericanstudies.org/,
keywords "1836 campaign"

Timeline of William Penn's life,
https://www.ushistory.org/penn/timeline.htm

Colonization Law Decree of 1823,
translated from the original Spanish,
http://www.sonsofdewittcolony.org/cololaws.htm#decree

Our Legacy—The Allen Brothers and Their Dream Town,
www.houstonhistory.com

The Texas State Historical Association's Handbook of Texas Online,
https://www.tshaonline.org/handbook

# About the Author

Betsy Wagner retired from a career in public education in 2008. It was then she discovered the interesting connections her family has with Texas' beginnings. She lives in Columbus, Texas, one of Stephen Austin's original pioneer communities. She works in partnership with her cousin Patricia Allen Duyfhuizen of Eau Claire, Wisconsin.

### Books by this author
*Spirit of Gonzales*
*Dauntless Spirit*
*Leland Comes To Stay*

# Notes

# Notes

# Notes

# Notes

Made in the USA
Columbia, SC
04 October 2021